THE PERFECT STORY

A Dash of Romance Novella

By Heather J. James

Amethyst Rush Press

First Edition April 2016
Library of Congress Control Number: 2016905808
ISBN: 0692687068
ISBN-13: 978-0692687062

Seattle: the Emerald City, the Rain City, the Jet City, and the Coffee Capital of the World.

CHAPTER ONE

JESS STEPPED INSIDE the small emergency room and stopped abruptly. A few people waited in hard plastic chairs to her right, but what got Jess's attention were the two guards who stood firmly in front of the double doors straight ahead. They weren't your run of the mill security guards — these two were well-trained private security guards. Dressed all in black, they looked like they had forgotten long ago how to smile, and they carried actual guns. Serious business. At least she knew she was in the right place.

She really needed a different job.

After five years of writing for several different gossip columns, Jess was more than ready to move on. She wanted to make a name for herself as a serious journalist, to pay off her debts, and to live far away from her hometown.

And yet here she was, chasing another gossip story. She reminded herself that this was the one that would get her noticed. The girl she was following had left her music tour secretly to come here to Seattle. Rumors were that she was visiting a nearby university. Could she be leaving the music industry to go back to school? Jess's editor thought the story was worth flying her here and paying for her expenses in order to stay close to the popular singer.

What was she going to do now? There was no way she could get past real security guards. Jess had already tried to get information from the front desk clerk. But the young woman with the short blond hair had refused to confirm or deny if the young celebrity had been brought here after the boating accident on Lake Washington. Which Jess had watched in horror. She didn't think it was a life-threatening injury, possibly just a broken arm, but it might make finding her easier when she was released from the ER.

Jess walked outside and hailed a cab back to her hotel. I'm not giving up, she told herself, as she sunk back into the cracked leather seat. I'm just regrouping.

The hotel she was staying in was one of the few in the busy area and looked like a national treasure, covered in marble, bronze, and mirrors. It was the kind of place where the rich and popular stayed.

Jess's editor had complained loudly when he had to pay for her two-week stay here. But Jess had just grinned and reminded him that she needed to stay where the celebrities were, so she would have a better chance of running into the young singer.

She smiled as the elevator zipped her up to the fifth floor. Even the elevator was decadent with mirrors and gold trim.

This was what she wanted her life to be like now. It was what she deserved, wasn't it? It had been hard growing up in Nogales, Arizona. She had grown up poor and always wanting more. She wanted better clothes to wear to school and decent food to eat, but mostly she wanted her mother to get her life together so Jess didn't have to be the adult.

Jess let herself into her room. Now, this was her idea of heaven. Her bed made every morning, mints on her pillow, and newly bleached white towels hung over the tiled soaker tub. She peered out her window at the jagged skyline of downtown Seattle in the distance and imagined herself traveling all over the world interviewing important people and staying in fancy hotels. She could set her own schedule, visit museums and shopping centers, and then go back to her luxurious hotel to type up stories.

This dream was what kept her going. Tomorrow she would check back at the hospital, but tonight she was going to blend into the wealthy staying here at the hotel. Maybe she would get lucky and run into another story.

The new skinny jeans and her favorite lavender blouse would fit in with the lounge crowd and have the added benefit of being comfortable. Sighing, she slipped on her flats, then grabbed her hotel key and cell phone. The door closed behind her with a soft click, and she double-checked to be certain it had locked.

As she rode the elevator to the rooftop lounge, she reflected on her conversation with David, the front desk clerk. According to him, the hotel was extra full this week, and she planned to find out what was going on as she worked the crowd in the lounge tonight. Lounges and bars were perfect places to meet people and stumble upon local gossip.

The elevator glided to a stop and the mirrored doors whooshed open. The large, dimly lit large room was already full of people drinking and laughing. She scanned the crowd as she made her way to the bar. Several well-dressed young men sat cheerfully drinking and enjoying the attention of giggling and attentive women. None of the men looked familiar, so they weren't actors or athletes. She knew just about everyone famous, at least by sight. With this job, lots of useless facts clogged up her brain.

It was tempting to join the intoxicated wealthy at one of the tables to eavesdrop to see what everyone was celebrating. She could turn any rumor into a story, with the right twist.

Jess shook her head, disgusted with herself, and turned away from the tables of laughing celebrants. She was here to find a big story, not another one of her local tabloid gossip pieces. She went over to the bar and sat down, suddenly depressed. She was still thinking like a small town gossip columnist. She needed to think bigger if she was to get a big break.

The bartender came over and took her drink order. She ordered her favorite, a strawberry margarita. The one bright spot growing up near the border was the delicious Mexican food. And then when she became of age (all right, maybe a few years before), her strawberry margaritas went perfectly with the street tacos.

When she was halfway through her second drink, a man sat down next to Jess. She didn't pay any attention to him at first. Not until he ordered a strawberry margarita. That got her attention. She assumed with this crowd, everyone would be ordering wine or champagne. Amongst the fancy bottles of alcohol in front of the mirror, Jess watched her neighbor. A black T-shirt hugged his buff body, highlighting the muscles underneath. He wore a black baseball cap pulled low over blond hair.

Jess willed him to look up, interested in seeing what was below that cap.

Instead of looking up at the mirror, he looked sideways. Directly at her. Startled, Jess turned to look into the lightest pale blue eyes she'd ever seen. She found herself speechless, and worse she couldn't stop staring. He was gorgeous under that cap. His perfectly tanned skin and slight facial stubble made her heart skip a beat.

He narrowed his eyes at her, and then turned back to his drink.

Good grief, Jess chided herself. What's wrong with me? She took another drink of margarita and then turned back to him. "I'm sorry for staring. It's just your eyes. I've never seen that beautiful shade of blue outside of the pacific ocean." Jess bit her lip. That was possibly one of the stupidest sounding things she'd ever said in a bar, or anywhere for that matter. She should've just kept her mouth shut.

He didn't say anything, just stared at his drink. Jess couldn't see the expression beneath the shadow of his cap, but he was probably thinking she was another crazy stranger trying to hit on him. With his looks, he most likely got that a lot.

She pushed her drink away and stood up. "I'm sorry. I didn't mean that to sound so creepy. I'm usually much better with my words. It's just been a really bad day."

He placed a hand on her arm and smiled. "It's all right, I'm not offended. Please stay. It's just been one of those days for me too." He shrugged his shoulders, his muscles rippling through the tight T-shirt. "Looks like we have that in common, at least." His accent, which she didn't recognize right away, sent shivers down her spine.

Jess sat back down and tried not to notice how absolutely perfect his jeans had fit him. "I'm Jess Platten." She put her hand out.

He took her hand in his. He had soft, yet strong hands. "You can call me Logan. Nice to meet you, Jess."

Jess smiled at him, trying to ignore the way his blue eyes seemed to pierce straight through her. "I think maybe I'd better order an appetizer if I'm going to avoid saying anything else stupid tonight."

He laughed and withdrew his hand from hers. Her hand still tingled from his touch as he waved down the bartender and ordered them some nachos to share. "They go well with margaritas." He said, his eyes sparkling.

"What if I don't like nachos?" Jess teased as she stirred her drink.

His face was a mock expression of horror. "Not like nachos? Well then I'd have to find someone else to share them with." But he didn't look away from her.

She swallowed. His gaze was intense, like she was the only one in the room. She took another drink, trying to act as though she wasn't totally taken in by his charm.

The nachos came, and Jess was grateful for the perfect timing. She waved a chip toward the other patrons at the bar. "There wouldn't really have been anyone else to share them with anyway." Everyone else at the bar was male. She smiled as she popped a chip laden with guacamole into her mouth. "Guess you're stuck with me."

CHAPTER TWO

LOGAN LOOKED AROUND and nodded. "True. Guess so." He smiled and took a few chips. What was he doing? The only reason he came here tonight was to fulfill his social obligation for the university.

All the right people were in attendance, and he'd forced himself to chat them up, hiding his nerves behind an expensive glass of wine. Every time someone had touched him, he'd cringed. After an excruciating hour he was finally able to get away from the crowd and retreat to the bar. There was only so much socializing he could handle, and he was almost on overload tonight. It would've taken too much energy to make his way through the crowd again to leave the bar.

So why was he talking to this woman if he wanted to be alone? He looked at her as she sipped her margarita and kept an eye on the activity around her. She seemed perfectly content to sit and watch and not join in on the revelry.

"So why aren't you out there joining in on the parties tonight?" He gestured out toward the crowded tables. It was kind of strange that someone so beautiful wasn't part of the many celebrations going on.

"I'm just in town for work. What is all the celebrating for anyway?" Her eyes scan the crowd as she took another drink.

"You really don't know who these people are?" Logan turned his body to face her. "I guess I assumed everyone staying at this hotel were here for the competition."

A crease appeared between her eyebrows. "No, I don't recognize anyone here." She swiveled in her chair to get a better look at the crowd. "What competition?"

Logan smiled. "Only the biggest regional competition for aspiring chefs."

"Really? There's such a thing? What do they win?" Her eyes sparkled as she turned to face him.

His stomach tightened, and his mouth went dry under her intense gaze. He took a drink of his margarita before answering. "The grand prize is a full ride scholarship to Le Cordon Bleu culinary school here in Seattle. Second and third prize winners get half scholarships."

She narrowed her eyes. "Why is that such a big deal? Is it an expensive school?" She pointed over to one of the tables. "All these people already seem to have lots of money. They don't look like they need scholarships."

So, she'd noticed that too, he thought. Very observant. "You're correct, most of them don't need the full ride scholarship. But by winning, they get a huge status boost. Most of these chefs have been training for years to open their own five-star restaurants. Winning this contest is a guaranteed formula for success."

"I see." She looked out at the tables of men and women as if memorizing everything.

Logan enjoyed watching her face as she took in the busy room. She was absolutely stunning with her mocha skin and green eyes that shimmered beneath the bar lights. She seemed so fully alive, and Logan was immensely drawn to her.

She turned back, catching him watching her. She smiled unselfconsciously. "And you? Are you one of them? Are you in this contest?"

Logan shook his head. "Not this year. I did win second place a few years ago. I'll be graduating from school this year." He finished up the last of the nachos and pushed the plate away.

"Seriously? You did? Congratulations. That must've been very exciting." She turned so she was fully facing him, her knees touching his.

His palms started sweating. "It got me into the school, anyway. I work a side job to pay for the rest of what the scholarship doesn't." He frowned as he remembered that he had to work early in the morning.

"You don't seem excited about all this. How come you're not out there partying it up with them?" She didn't take her eyes off him, just nodded her head in the direction of the noise.

She really didn't miss anything. "I just don't fit in very well." He gave her a weak smile. "I'm not the social type. I made my rounds already since I know most of the people here and they expect it, but now I'm done for the night."

She laughed and briefly touched his arm, his skin warming under her touch. "And yet you're here socializing with me."

Logan felt his face grow warm. "One on one I can handle." He felt his face grow hot as he realized how that sounded. "What I mean is that I'm more comfortable around smaller groups of people." Logan wasn't sure what was wrong with him. He had just met this woman, and he was already tongue-tied.

She nodded. "I can identify with that. My job forces me to be social too, but I'm much happier by myself or out with just a few friends."

Logan sat up straight. "All this talk about the competition and I haven't even ask what you're here for. What kind of work do you do?"

Her smile dropped and she looked away. To Logan it seemed like the temperature of the room also dropped as her smile left. He immediately regretted asking the question.

"That's why I'm having such a bad day. I'm a freelance journalist, and the story I came here for hasn't worked out the way I planned." She watched the bartender hand more drinks to one of the waitresses.

"Freelance journalist? Like a reporter?" That set off warning bells.

She looked back at him. "Kind of. I'm trying to get a promotion to become a journalist for national magazine. Right now, I just write fluff stories – celebrity gossip, border issues, farming reports. Most of my articles are just sensationalist local gossip." She looked away. "That's why I really needed this story to be taken seriously by the magazine editors."

Logan swallowed and told himself he needed to end this conversation right now and go home. He couldn't have anyone poking around in his private life. Not this close to graduation. Especially someone as observant and intelligent as Jess seemed to be.

He stayed quiet and watched as she fidgeted with the straw in her drink. It was obvious that she was embarrassed by what she just shared with him. Logan realized she'd just trusted him with something very delicate and personal. This made her even more attractive and caused him to stay glued to his chair even though he should've rushed for the exit.

Despite his better judgment and the danger this beautiful woman represented, he decided that he wanted to know more about her. He told himself he would just be careful. Just one conversation at a bar couldn't hurt anything.

CHAPTER THREE

JESS COULDN'T BELIEVE she had just told Logan about the whole gossip column thing. If she was going to leave the past behind, this wasn't the way to do it. What if he found out exactly the kind of stories she wrote? No one wanted to talk to or be seen with trash reporters. Good job, Jess. Way to scare off yet another handsome guy.

She looked up from her empty glass and caught him staring at her, wearing a guarded expression. She groaned. "I know. It's a horrible way to make a living. Even though it pays the bills, it's still embarrassing."

Logan shook his head. "I'm not judging you. I figure we all need to go through jobs that maybe aren't quite so glamorous, so that when the good jobs do come around we'll appreciate them. I think it was very brave of you to share that with me." He gave her a big smile, and motioned to the bar tender for his tab.

Jess's insides warmed at his words. "Thank you. I appreciate that. Although it might not be bravery on my part." She turned her head to the side, still keeping her eyes on him. "It might just be the margaritas."

He laughed and slapped down money on the bar for their drinks and nachos. "Whatever the reason, it was really nice talking with you tonight. It's refreshing having a conversation that doesn't have to do with the competition." He took his hat off and ran his fingers through his hair. "I have to work early in the morning, but maybe we could meet again for lunch tomorrow?"

Jess gave a little smile as she tried to hide her delight. His body language was relaxed, but his eyes still gave away his nervousness. I guess I didn't scare him off quite yet. But he was still holding back.

She pretended to get serious. "I don't know. Where would we go that a famous chef from Le Cordon Bleu school would approve of?" The alcohol had made her relaxed and flirty. Too bad he had to go already, she was actually enjoying herself.

He stood up and helped her off the stool. "I'm sure we can find someplace I won't object to." He winked at her, making her stomach flutter. She fumbled trying to retrieve her purse from the back of the barstool.

Logan reached across her and helped her unwind it from the wire-backed stool. She inhaled his scent of fresh soap and just a hint of cologne. She was suddenly very warm.

He looked up at her, their faces just inches apart. "Here you go." His voice was husky, barely a whisper as he handed over her purse.

"Thank you," she managed to say. She stepped back, putting some distance between them so maybe she would stop acting like an idiot.

He nodded toward the elevator. "Why don't I walk you to your room on my way out? You're staying here, right?"

"Yes, I am." Jess looked around to get her bearings. She was feeling lightheaded, and it wasn't from the alcohol. "On the fifth floor." She started toward the elevators, trying to find the best way to get through the throng of people.

Logan took her arm and pulled her toward the edge of the room. He then placed his hand on the small of her back and guided her around the perimeter, avoiding most of the crowd. Jess had to concentrate on walking, as she was all too aware of the heat of his hand.

He didn't take his hand away until they found an empty elevator and stepped in. Jess laughed and leaned against the mirrored elevator wall. "It's nice being around someone that dislikes crowds as much as I do."

He relaxed beside her and smiled. They looked at each other in the mirror across from them. Jess smiled at his reflection. "All those people seem to know you and really want your attention. Yet, here you are leaving the party early to walk me to my door. There must be more to your story than just winning a scholarship. They seem to want something from you. I think I can guess at least what the women want from you." She raised an eyebrow at him. "But what about the men?"

He laughed. "It's not what you think. And it's not as flattering as all that." He shook his head.

"Okay, so if it's not for your gorgeous surfer boy looks and amazing accent, what is it that they want from you?" She blushed, realizing too late she actually said all that out loud.

He grinned at her. "Surfer boy?"

Jess rolled her eyes wishing she could hide somewhere. "I blame it on the margaritas."

"And you think my accent is amazing?" He was still grinning, enjoying Jess's discomfort. "I forget sometimes that I have an accent. It's only been two years since I left South Africa."

Jess nodded, trying to figure out some way to salvage some dignity. "That's what your accent is, I couldn't place it. Just forget I said most of that and just answer the question." She turned slightly so she was face to face with him.

"Right." He hesitated. Jess wasn't sure if he was going to answer so she placed her hand on his arm to encourage him.

He swallowed and looked at her hand curved around his forearm. "I'm one of the judges for the competition. They don't really want to know me — they just want to be on my good side. They want me to like them and show them favoritism." He frowned, a crease showing between his eyebrows.

The elevator doors opened, but they didn't move. Jess squeezed his arm and then removed her hand. "No wonder you avoid crowds. I'm sorry, it must be hard to figure out who your true friends are in that kind of situation."

Logan forced a smile. "At least this will be my last year as a judge." He stepped out of the elevator.

She wasn't convinced by his attempt at a lighthearted answer, but she didn't press. She started down the hallway thinking how similar their social lives were. In her line of work, there were no friends either. Only friendly acquaintances and people she needed information from, or they needed something from her.

He was quiet beside her. She bumped her shoulder into his to get his attention. "So what will you do after graduation? Open up your own restaurant or cooking school?"

He shook his head sadly. "Honestly, I'm not sure what I want to do after graduation." He looked over at her and gave a small shrug. "That's why I came here, to learn to run my own restaurant. But I'm not so sure what I want to do anymore." His gaze got distant, and he shoved his hands into his jean pockets. "I do enjoy creating new recipes, I'm just not sure I want to cook in an actual restaurant."

Jess thought he looked so sad and lost for someone who seemed so successful. This was something that was really tearing him up inside. He's lost his passion. She'd seen this many times before. Celebrities and athletes who had been in the spotlight for a long time, eventually questioned why they were still working so hard at it. It took more than money and fame to be happy. They realized they needed passion driving them or it wasn't worth it. The ones who lost their passion made for the best stories in her line of work.

CHAPTER FOUR

LOGAN HADN'T TOLD anyone before how unsure he was about his future. His family was set on him starting his own restaurant back home. With graduation coming up, he would need to decide soon.

Jess turned to him, her green eyes pinning him in place. "If you don't want to cook anymore, what do you think you want to do?"

Logan slowly smiled. He had expected her to come down on him like his family and friends did. When he would try expressing his frustrations to them, they always just told him how talented he was and how much of a waste it would be not to use his expensive education back in South Africa. Like he owed his success to his country or his parents. It made him miserable because he knew they were right, in a way. He had come here for this education, and it was worth every penny. But that didn't stop the doubts from plaguing him.

"You mean you're not going to tell me that I'd be stupid to waste all this?" Logan smiled and opened his arms to take in the lush surroundings.

Jess shook her head. "No. I don't think your education would be wasted even if you decided to become a carpenter or real estate agent. The time you spent learning to cook and the business of restaurants will never be wasted. It's still part of who you are." She stepped closer and placed her hand on his chest, sending heat waves throughout his body.

Logan took in a quick breath. "You're the only one who thinks that." He met her gaze. "My family already thinks I'm on the wrong path and so do most of my friends here at the university." Logan reached up and placed his hand over hers and squeezed it.

Jess looked at their clasped her hands and cleared her throat. "I should probably get going. You have an early day, and I still need to figure out what I'm going to do for a story." She tilted her head up and smiled.

Afraid of how much his body was responding to her touch, Logan let go of her hand and started toward her room. "Yes, I do have an early day tomorrow." He hoped she wouldn't turn her investigative eye on him and realize what kind of effect she was having on him.

They walked in silence. At her door, Logan hesitated. "I did enjoy our time tonight. It was nice getting to know you, Jess." He studied her face wondering what she was thinking.

Jess threw her head back and laughed. "That sounds more like a farewell than a 'let's have lunch.'"

Flustered, Logan stammered, "No, I didn't mean it to sound that way. I do want to have lunch with you." He frowned. "Sorry, I'm better at cooking than with words. I just meant that it was nice talking to someone who wasn't only trying to gain my vote."

Jess nodded and started fumbling through her purse to find her room key. As she slipped it out, she looked up and smiled at him. "It really was a nice evening for me too. One of the best I've had in awhile, actually. Besides, I can't wait to see where Chef Logan will take me to lunch tomorrow."

Logan shook his head. "So much pressure. I'm going to have to think hard about this so I don't disappoint."

Jess laughed lightly. Logan enjoyed that sound and was tempted to keep the conversation going longer, despite the late hour.

"I'm sure I'll enjoy anyplace you think is a decent meal. You do have great taste in drinks." She opened her door and stood there, one hand on the door, a mischievous smile playing on her full lips. For a brief moment, he wondered what it would be like to kiss her.

Before he could act on his curiosity, she leaned in and kissed him on the cheek, freezing him in place. "I'll meet you downstairs around noon?"

Heart thudding in his chest, Logan could only nod as she shut the door.

He stared at her door trying to figure out if he felt disappointed or relieved that things didn't go further than a kiss on the cheek. He smiled to himself and headed toward the elevator. Here he was telling himself he shouldn't get involved with her, but at the same time, he wanted nothing more than to kiss her goodnight. He shook his head and berated himself all the way down the elevator.

He lived just a few miles from the hotel, so he decided to walk home, instead of taking a cab. It was a warm evening, the air heavy with coming rain. The farther he got from the hotel, the more he felt they had done the right thing tonight by not taking it any further.

Logan wasn't one of those one-night stand kind of guys. He never had been. But it had sure crossed his mind tonight. Why was he so drawn to this woman he had just met?

That was another problem. Why her? He'd finally met a woman who was smart and beautiful, someone he got along with, and her job could ruin everything for him. She was a danger with her curiosity and her need for a story. He couldn't afford to have her digging into his past. He was confused enough about his future to have his past come back to haunt him.

He really shouldn't go to lunch with her. He needed to just concentrate on this last week of school, and getting through this last competition. He had enough on his plate; he didn't need any more distractions. And she was a very tempting distraction.

By the time he got back to his small apartment, he had decided he would show up tomorrow and tell her he couldn't do lunch. It wasn't like he would ever see her again, he reasoned.

After she found some story or other, she would be returning home.

He fell into bed, his mind struggling to come up with a way to get out of lunch with such an amazing woman. He was so confused. On one hand, he really wanted to get to know her better. He hadn't ever met a woman so comfortable with herself, or full of passion and curiosity. On the other hand, those same intelligent qualities could get him in a lot of trouble. As hard as he tried, he couldn't push her out of his thoughts and dreams.

CHAPTER FIVE

JESS DIDN'T SLEEP well. Not only did she desperately need to find a career-changing story within a week, but she couldn't get Logan and his incredible ocean blue eyes out of her head. She had tossed and turned trying to figure out what to do about both dilemmas.

Groaning, she forced herself to roll out of bed around five in the morning. Every muscle in her body ached with exhaustion as she stumbled across the room. Steam filled the bathroom quickly as Jess set the shower to the hottest she could stand. As the cascade of scalding water hit her back, she put the surfer boy chef with the mesmerizing eyes out of her mind. Somehow, she had to shift her concentration to her career.

Meeting him for lunch was out; she didn't have time. She needed to track down that diva, or figure out another amazing story that would get her away from the life back home.

Rinsing the soap off her body, she considered her options. There had to be lots of stories to be uncovered in a city of this size. As her hands ran over the thin scars on her thighs, she was reminded again why she didn't need to be getting close to a man right now. She leaned her head against the wall of the shower and allowed the spray to cover her. The physical scars were starting to fade, but the mental ones remained, always to put a damper on her happiness.

When the water ran cold, she turned it off and stepped out to dry off. As she stared at her reflection in the mirror, she forced herself to think toward the future and mentally pictured herself succeeding. The past was not worth dwelling on, and she had a job to do.

Jess put on a casual outfit that showed off her curves, yet hid the scars. She did minimal makeup and put her hair up in a ponytail. She wanted to talk with the hotel staff to see if anyone had seen her news story diva. Even in a town this size the porters and housekeepers in the different hotels would have communication with each other. If someone had seen her anywhere in town, the staff would know.

Jess was an expert at blending in and making friends quickly. That was why she was so good at her job. She had used this trait to get and keep anonymous sources for her articles. Hotel staff always knew what went on in their hotels but they valued their jobs, so she was adamant about keeping their identities secret. She couldn't sacrifice someone else's livelihood for her own gain. Although she knew many reporters who did, Jess had promised herself she would never be like them.

When the elevator stopped at the ground floor, she got off and wandered over to the dining area. Several wealthy couples sat sipping Mimosas and eating breakfast. She recognized many faces from last night at the bar, although it was a much more subdued crowd this morning.

The waiters and bus staff were quietly slipping in and out of double doors near the back of the room. Just as she neared the doors they swung open, startling her.

A tall waiter with his arms loaded with a heavy tray came through in a hurry. She held the door so it didn't swing back and knock the dishes out of his hands.

He nodded to her. "Thank you," and hustled out to the dining room.

Jess slipped into the kitchen and looked around. Chefs stood over steaming pans and hot stoves in the center of the room, and waiters rushed in from time to time to grab plates from the warming counter. Jess skirted around the side of the kitchen, careful to stay out of everyone's way.

At the back of the kitchen, two petite girls with pink faces loaded dirty dishes into a giant commercial dishwasher. As Jess approached, they looked up but didn't stop working.

"Hi, my name is Jess. I'm sorry to bother you, but I was wondering if you could help me with something?" She plastered on her most innocent smile and continued before they could say anything. "My employer requested me to set up a special reception party at a hotel, but I think I wrote down the wrong place." Jess described the blond singer and shook her head sadly. "I thought for sure it would be this hotel, but they said at the front desk she has no reservations here, and all the rooms are already reserved for some other big function."

The girls looked at each other, obviously recognizing who Jess was talking about. The tallest one dried her hands and turned around to face Jess. She was very pretty, even with her hair pulled back and her face sweaty and flushed from the heat of the hot water.

"She's not at any of the hotels that we know of." With a shrug, she looked at the shorter girl. "Most of the hotels are full because of the cooking competition. Keeps us busy with all the university students and rich people coming in at all hours." She blew a stray hair out of her face. Her hair net was loose and her uniform was disheveled. It looked like she'd been on her feet for days.

"Are there any other places someone like her would stay? I doubt she would just stay anywhere, and I don't think she knows anyone in this city." She relaxed into the role, grateful that these two had accepted her. To Jess, this was a truer role for her to play than the rich reporter living it up in a fancy hotel room. "I'm not ready to tell her I made a mistake yet. You know?" She lowered her head and looked down at the wet, greasy floor.

"You might want to ask around at the university where the cooking contest is being held." Jess looked into the dark brown eyes of the shorter girl, her arms still deep in suds. "Most of the hotel guests are here for the contest, so someone at the school might've seen her. She could be staying on campus

20

somewhere. I know who she is, but we haven't seen her around here." She smiled at Jess and then went back to her task.

Jess thanked the girls and made her way back out of the kitchen. This was twice now that she heard about the cooking competition. Maybe meeting Logan wasn't such a dilemma after all. He might be the way to find her story.

At the front of the hotel, the doorman greeted her warmly as he opened the door for her. She stepped outside and was assaulted by the strong scent of too many people, car fumes, and a strange mixture of food smells.

She walked for about an hour to clear her head and get her bearings around the neighborhood surrounding the hotel. She found the university where the cooking competition would be held but shied away from exploring the campus. She made a mental note to visit there after lunch.

This was also most likely the university the singer was rumored to be checking out, so her story wasn't lost yet. The beautiful girl should be easy to spot since she probably wore a cast or sling on her arm from the boating accident.

A familiar twinge of guilt twisted in her belly. Once again, she would have to use someone to get her story. Even though she had just met Logan, she still felt bad. This wouldn't hurt him, she told herself. The story wasn't about him — she just needed access to the university. And maybe in the meantime they could have some fun. Jess continued to argue with herself during the walk back to the hotel.

She hurried to the elevator. Logan would be here soon to take her to lunch. Once in her room she changed into a lacy top and fitted Capris. She checked her makeup and hurried downstairs to find Logan waiting in the lobby, chatting with the desk clerk.

Leaning against the counter, he looked like a model confidently posing for a California beach magazine. He wore khakis that fit him way too well, and a button-up shirt. Jess groaned inwardly as she stared at his tanned skin contrasting nicely with his white shirt. He was actually much better looking than any of the models she'd ever seen, with that crazy sexy yet down-to-earth air about him.

She took a deep breath to get her thoughts (and hormones) under control. She was just going to lunch with him, and maybe obtain information that would help pursue her story. She couldn't afford to get sidetracked by his extreme good looks. This day was going to take some extra self-control, and Jess hoped she was up for the challenge.

CHAPTER SIX

LOGAN CAUGHT SIGHT of Jess out of the corner of his eye and was immediately distracted, completely missing what the desk clerk was telling him. He apologized and excused himself to meet Jess near the front doors.

She was stunning, and all thoughts of canceling lunch flew out of his mind.

"Hi." Logan said as they met in the middle of the foyer. "You look great."

"Thanks. You clean up pretty good yourself. Especially considering you had a late night at the bar and then an early morning at work." She smiled, sending Logan's stomach flipping. "I pretty much need a solid seven hours of sleep."

Logan could feel his skin getting hot and tried not to think about Jess sleeping. "You ready for lunch?"

"Yes, starving." She turned toward the front door and Logan fell into step beside her. She looked at him sideways. "Are you going to tell me where we're going?"

Logan laughed. "That would ruin the surprise, don't you think?"

"Yes, but how do I know I'm dressed appropriately for wherever we're going then?" Jess greeted the doorman by name as he held the door for them. Logan nodded as they walked by.

Outside, Logan waved down a cab. To Jess he said, "You're dressed perfectly for where we're going. Trust me." Then he winked as he opened the door of the cab for her.

She smiled back at him, blushing.

He gave the driver the address to the restaurant and sat back in the seat, shoulder to shoulder with Jess. Heat radiated from her, and the smell of jasmine wafted on the air. A good chef knew the scents of every ingredient in a dish. Logan had always had a discerning nose, which helped him exceed at cooking.

Jess turned slightly to face him, encouraging more of the enticing scent. "So how was your morning? Do you always work so early?"

"Yes, I'm the prep chef. I do all the cutting and chopping early in the morning, and then I have my classes in the afternoon." He was impressed he could still sound coherent as his pulse quickened in response to her proximity.

"Is that where we're going for lunch?" She raised her eyebrows at him.

Logan narrowed his eyes at her. She was quick. "It's not fancy, but they do have the best tacos in the whole city." He frowned. "You do like Mexican food, right? I guess I should've asked first. So much for that surprise." Logan chided himself for not thinking things through a little better.

Jess laughed and her eyes lit up. "Yes, I do. You'll find I'm pretty easy to please when it comes to food. As long as I don't have to cook it." She placed her hand on his knee causing his body to flush warm again. "I admire you for your talent in cooking. My cooking can barely be considered edible."

"I'm sure it's not that bad." It was difficult to concentrate on their conversation when her touch was driving him crazy.

"Yes, yes it's that bad. I have to drink several glasses of wine just to get through cooking a meal, because I already know it's going to be awful."

"Really? Do you use recipes? And they still don't turn out?" Logan smiled, amused.

Jess nodded, a serious look on her face. "Yes, I totally follow the recipes. But it never turns out right anyway."

Logan looked out the window. They were stopped in the heavy Seattle traffic, cars inching along, pedestrians weaving through the downtown traffic. "Maybe you just didn't have the right teacher." He looked back at her.

She smiled. "Are you offering to teach me to cook?" Her eyes seemed to drill into the very center of Logan. He squirmed under her gaze.

"Only if you want me to. I know we've just met and you still have a job to do." Why had he offered that? He was supposed to just have lunch with her and then put distance between them.

A police car drew up beside them with its siren blaring, making it impossible for Jess to answer. While they waited for it to make its way past their traffic jam, Logan looked out the window again and tried to get his thoughts off how he could feel every point where her body touched his.

People were hurrying along the sidewalk, heads bent down, not looking at one another. The Space Needle peeked through the buildings ahead of them as a shining beacon of light, but where they were stopped there was nothing but run down shops and warehouses. This part of town was not for tourists.

No one paid attention to a skinny little boy all by himself near the alley entrance or the old man who sat in an abandoned doorway with his arms wrapped tightly around himself. The people just hurried on by. Logan closed his eyes, frustrated and heartbroken by the sight, and the feeling of being unable to help them.

The siren finally faded away, and Logan felt Jess's warm hand squeeze his knee to get his attention. He looked at her. She had concerned on her face as she gazed up at him.

Logan waved out the window at the masses of people. "It just gets to me, seeing so many people not enjoying life, and not taking care of those that need help." He pointed out the little boy who was now heading down the dirty alley. He shook his head. "But I'm sure you don't want to hear my frustrations with society. Sorry about that." He gave her a weak smile.

"Actually, it's refreshing being with someone who cares." The cab started forward with a slight lurch and Jess put out her arms to brace herself against the seat in front of her.

Logan instantly missed the warmth of her hand on his knee.

She settled back into the seat again. "So, the answer to your question, whether you were being serious or not, is yes. I would love to take cooking lessons from you under one condition." She grinned.

Logan's heart skipped a beat. What could he do against that smile? "What's your condition?"

"You have to promise not to take it personally when you fail to make a decent cook out of me." Her laughter made Logan's stomach flutter.

"I don't think you could be that bad. Really."

She scowled at him.

"Okay, okay, I promise." Anything to remain close to her. Logan decided his body had won out over his mind. He was in so much trouble.

CHAPTER SEVEN

THE CAB DEPOSITED them in front of a brightly painted building in a rough-looking neighborhood. Several closed businesses lined the road on both sides of the restaurant, their boarded-up doors and windows colored in graffiti. Here and there, patches of weeds grew from cracks in the sidewalk. They weren't very far from the lush university campus, but this area seemed like another world altogether. Jess frowned and looked at Logan who had just finished paying the cab driver.

He shrugged. "I know it doesn't look like much, but I promise the food is amazing. You still up for this?" Concern showed on his handsome features.

Jess put her arm through his. "Of course. I'm just shocked that this is where you would come eat, Mr. Fancy Chef."

"And work. Five days a week." He grinned.

She gave him a crooked smile and tugged him toward the entrance. They weaved around the people waiting outside. Although it was lightly sprinkling, there was quite a line hunkered underneath the awnings waiting for a table inside.

They stepped inside, and the smell of cooking pork, onions and cilantro hit Jess and made her stomach growl. She hoped Logan couldn't hear it over all the noise.

The restaurant was opposite of the neighborhood outside. Inside it was clean, bright and cheery. Modern light fixtures lit up colorful murals painted with flowers and dancers among snaking ivy. Jess smiled to herself as she thought of all the new places like this she would discover when she was a successful news journalist.

He gave his name to the hostess, and they moved to the bar to wait for a table. Using perfect Spanish, Logan ordered margaritas for them both.

Jess smiled at him. His already sexy South African accent was even more amazing when he spoke Spanish. "How many languages do you know, anyway?"

"Just three. My native language of Afrikaans, Spanish, and English. It comes in handy when I want to impress a beautiful woman." He shrugged and gave her a crooked grin.

Jess laughed. "And just how many women have you brought here? And did you actually get them to come in the door? It's a pretty rough-looking neighborhood."

Logan looked up at the ceiling as if counting, a serious look on his face.

Jess smacked his arm, making him smile. She really liked that smile.

His grin returned. "Honestly, you're the first. I don't really have time for a social life, and most of the women I know from the university wouldn't come to a place like this. They would be afraid of getting out of the cab in this neighborhood."

"And how did you know I would get out of the cab?" Jess asked.

He turned toward her and smiled. "I knew you were up to the challenge and—"

"—because I'm a low-life gossip journalist? That I'd feel right at home in a neighborhood that looks like this?" She cringed at how biting that sounded.

Logan's smile faded. "No, I don't think of you like that at all. I think you're a strong, passionate woman who can see past the tough exteriors and notice what's really important inside. You and your instincts are anything but low-life, Jess."

Jess bit her lip. "I'm sorry. I shouldn't have jumped to conclusions." She looked around. "I'm so used to seeing successful men like you looking down on people like me. Writing me off as lower class."

Logan let out a bitter laugh. "I'm not quite the success I seem." He shook his head. "And I definitely don't see you as anything other than beautiful and successful. I don't think you've been hanging around the right kind of people."

Jess smiled. How true. She definitely hadn't been around the right kind of people.

The hostess came and led them to a table that was tucked back into an intimate corner of the restaurant, away from the noise of the main crowd. Jess smiled at Logan as they sat down. "This is nice. Your usual table?" Red light bathed us from a neon Tecate sign and Mariachi music played over speakers hidden behind greenery decorating high shelves.

Logan nodded. "I deal with people all day long. When I come here to eat, I want to just enjoy the food. It's my comfort zone." He looked fondly around the busy room.

A waiter came over and brought them salsa and chips. Logan and the waiter had a good-natured conversation in Spanish while he took their order.

Jess's stomach growled again so she dug into the chips and salsa. "Mmmm. This is delicious. I haven't had salsa this good in a long time. My grandma use to make several batches every summer, and I would eat chips and homemade salsa all winter." Jess scooped up another bite of salsa.

Logan grinned at her. "Wait until you taste the tacos. Enrique does an amazing job." He looked around at the waiters rushing back and forth and the tables full of food. "People come from all over the city to eat his famous tacos."

"I'm looking forward to it." Jess smiled, relaxing a bit. "And I'm sorry again for being defensive earlier."

"Don't worry about it. I didn't explain myself very well." He shrugged.

Jess looked away. "No, it's not your fault. I've just had a rough couple of years. I know people don't think much of my profession, but where I come from there are far worse things a girl can do to make a living." Jess looked back at Logan and studied his face. He didn't seem to be judging her, so she kept going. "My mom was the only African American professor at the University of Phoenix in Nogales where I grew up. She fell in love with one of her white students and got pregnant with me. His family was very influential at the university and didn't like their son getting involved with her, so they found a way to fire her. After that, the only jobs Mom could find in a town like Nogales were less than desirable. The best one was at the local grocery store. But she became depressed and turned to drugs. She was a semi-functional drug addict who was barely able to take care of herself, let alone me. I was determined to get out of there. One of my high school teachers helped me get grants for a college a few towns away. I was at least able to get an education and get away from most of the bad influences that were in my life." Jess finished off her margarita.

Logan waved a waiter over and ordered her another drink. "What do you mean by you got away from most of the bad influences? You couldn't get away from all of them?"

Jess munched on a few chips before she answered. "No. One of the guys I dated for awhile followed me, basically stalking me, and harassing my roommate until I agreed to move back in with him. He'd rented a rundown apartment and we lived off my student loans. He never did get a job." Jess closed her eyes. How could she have let herself get into that situation? She never stopped kicking herself for being so weak. When Jess opened her eyes again, Logan was watching her quietly. She offered a weak smile. "I managed to at least finish my degree despite all of that."

Logan reached over and squeezed her hand. "I'm sorry you had to go through all that. Was he abusive?" His blue eyes were intense and Jess squirmed in her seat. She tried to pull her hand away, but Logan gently kept hold of it.

Jess felt herself shrinking into her chair. "Once I graduated, I was offered a job immediately at a regional newspaper. But it was about eight hours away, and he didn't want me to take it. We argued, and I ended up in the emergency room for a few days." Jess looked away as the nightmare threatened to surface again. She blinked a few times before continuing. "The hospital staff helped me sneak out and catch a bus out of town before he could come get me. I arrived in a new city with just the borrowed clothes that I wore out of the hospital. I changed my name and learned to blend into a new life. That talent made me very good at my job at the gossip magazine."

Logan stayed silent, rubbing his thumb over her hand. It sent shivers down her spine.

"Anyway, that's why I'm so determined to get a big story. If I can write an important enough article, the larger newspapers will have to take me seriously. Then I can stop pretending to be someone I'm not." She smiled at him.

The waiter came, and Logan released her hand. Although she was disappointed they were interrupted, she enjoyed the huge smile on his face when the waiter placed warm plates of tacos in front of them.

After the waiter cleared the dishes, Logan leaned forward, his voice quiet. "So, Jess, is this the real you tonight, or are you someone else when you're with me?"

Jess's stomach did a flip-flop. His gaze was intense, questioning. How could she answer him, when she didn't even know who the real Jess was? She shrugged her shoulders. "I feel comfortable with you, like I don't have to hide anything. I've never told anyone outside my family the story of why I changed my name. Truthfully, it's been a very long time since I didn't have to pretend, so I'm not really sure who I am anymore." She frowned and hoped he'd understand.

Logan stared at her for a heartbeat. Then as if he'd come to some sort of decision, his body relaxed and he nodded at her. "Thank you for sharing your story with me. I appreciate you trusting me with it."

Trust was new to Jess, and Logan's statement made her feel warm all the way down to her toes. She stared at his lips and imagined kissing him.

A crash of glass behind the bar brought her attention back to reality. Jess felt the loss of the imagined kiss.

Logan signaled the waiter for their check. "Would you like a tour of the university? Maybe we'll end up finding your story after all?" His smile was heart stopping and his tone hopeful. How could anyone ever say no to him?

"Yes I'd like that. I had planned on scouting out the area anyway. Someone's got to have seen her." Jess said, thinking about her lead from the hotel kitchen staff.

Logan paid for their meal and led them out through the maze of tables. His hand was warm on the small of her back, making a delicious shiver travel up Jess's spine. What am I doing? Jess chided herself. I've got to stay focused, and this is definitely not the way to do it.

Once in the cab, Jess tried to maintain some distance between them to calm her desire for his touch. To divert her attention, Jess thought of her tiny rundown apartment back home, bare and dingy. She tried to hold onto that image to keep her focus. She had to write this story. She could do this. She would get her story and then later figure out what this was between her and Logan.

CHAPTER EIGHT

SITTING THIS CLOSE to Jess was testing Logan's self-control. He wanted to touch her soft skin and kiss her full lips. It was getting harder to keep from giving in to those desires the more time he spent with her. She had bared her secrets to him. There was no way he would be able to break things off now. He was hooked. He groaned inwardly, knowing he was making a big mistake but couldn't do anything about it. Or didn't want to do anything about it.

The cab turned down a street lined with old maple trees. It was the beginning of fall, and the magnificent trees wore leaves in different shades of orange, red, and yellow. Logan smiled. He loved it here at the university. The acres of historic buildings were surrounded by gardens and a variety of trees. It was peaceful living here.

Logan looked at Jess. She looked enraptured at the view, her curiosity and passion shining through her eyes. His heart swelled with feelings for this woman. He hoped that they could find the girl Jess was after. Then she would have a story to pursue and they could keep enjoying lunch dates like this.

Logan wondered, though, even if Jess got the journalism job, would he ever feel free around her? She could expose him at anytime. Was it worth it to get to know her better?

Logan broke off his chain off thought before he could dwell on it further. Just live in the moment, appreciate the here and now, Logan reminded himself. That was why he was here, to make his own choices and enjoy life free from his oppressive family.

He pointed to a newer building that they were passing. "The cooking school is at the far side of the university. But the actual competition will take place here in the auditorium. It's set up for video and a good size audience."

"Its modern look is out of place among these older brick buildings." Jess pointed to the other side of the street where old brick and stone rectangle buildings stood.

"Yes, there's quite the diversity in architecture here. The newer buildings are quite obvious." Logan watched several students carrying backpacks and coffee cups rush down the sidewalk.

Jess turned to Logan, her shoulder brushing against his briefly. "So where did you grow up, Logan? Before you moved to Washington."

Logan's heart skipped a beat. Jess had confided in him, but did he dare do the same? "I'm from outside Cape Town originally. I moved to the U.S. the day after I turned eighteen."

"With your parents?"

"No, just me. I moved to San Diego first before I moved up here for chef school. I ate at Enrique's so often when I first lived here, that he decided to hire me." Logan smiled as he thought how much he owed to Enrique. "Without Enrique, I would've been swallowed up by this city."

"So you worked your way through chef school? Between your job and the partial scholarship is how you paid for all this?" Jess gestured out the window.

Logan felt his cheeks burning. "Not exactly. Yes, I worked the whole time I've been going to school. I didn't want my family paying for my schooling." He looked out the window.

Jess reached over and placed her hand on his arm. "I'm sorry, I shouldn't have asked about finances. It just looks like this place would be expensive to attend."

Logan turned back to look at Jess. "It's all right. I just don't like to talk about my family since I moved here to get away from them." The familiar guilt weighed Logan down as he admitted this out loud.

Jess shook her head. "You shouldn't be so hard on yourself. There are no normal families." Jess gave a small smile and pulled her hand back.

Logan immediately felt the loss of contact. "Jess, I—"

The cab stopped just then, breaking Logan's thought. He scrambled to pay the driver as Jess climbed out the other door.

The cab left, and Logan and Jess stood in front of a three-story brick building. Students were going in and out, some of them wearing white chef jackets.

Logan waved at a few students before he turned back to Jess. "Ready for the tour? We can start here at the culinary building and then work our way over to the admin building where you can see if they can help you find your mystery girl." Logan shrugged his shoulders and took a step toward the building. "Maybe you'll get lucky and someone there will have seen her."

Jess grinned at him. "Sounds good. Lead on."

"Let's stop up at my office so I can grab my keys, in case they have the kitchens locked up."

Logan led her in the main doors and through the crowd of students.

"Most of the cooking classes are in the morning, and then they head to the other buildings for their core classes," Logan explained.

"Don't you have any classes today?"

"No, I only have final exams left. Next week." Logan grimaced as he thought of the studying he still had to do this weekend. "My exams are earlier than most of the students because I'm a judge in the competition. I'm expected to help organize all the details of the competition."

Logan led them over to a wide staircase that was worn from many years of use. They walked up one flight and came to a hallway that looked like it ran the length of the whole building.

"There are so many classrooms. I could get lost here." Jess squeezed close to Logan to let a few students pass them.

Logan chuckled. "I did all the time my first year here. The second and third floors are also classrooms and offices, so they all look like alike."

Soon they were the only ones left in the hallway, and their footsteps echoed off the walls.

Jess peeked into a few of the empty classrooms as they passed by. "My college was an even smaller campus than this. We didn't have anything quite this large."

"On the fourth floor we have the larger lecture hall. Most of the first year classes are taught there. By second and third year there aren't as many students, so they use these classrooms."

"Why aren't there as many returning students? Are the classes that hard?"

"Yep. That first year they really try to weed out students who aren't serious about cooking. Most of the professors who teach the upper level classes are already famous chefs with busy restaurants to run. They want dedicated students so they don't feel like they're wasting their time here. So they expect a lot out of their students." Logan grinned as he watched Jess's curious eyes take in everything around them.

Logan turned them down a narrow hallway almost hidden at the end of a row of classrooms. They passed several offices when they heard people talking. Logan stopped in his tracks.

Jess stumbled as she came to a stop beside him. "What's the matter, Logan?"

Logan's skin grew cold as he listened to the familiar voices. He had to get Jess out of there right away.

"Is there someone in your office?" Jess asked.

Logan looked ahead at the opaque door with his name written in black letters. Silhouettes of two people moved around inside.

Logan took a deep breath and nodded. "My parents." This could very well be the worst possible time for his parents to show up. Figured. He'd never be free from them.

"Really? That's great, right?" Jess frowned. "You don't seem so excited to see them." She looked over at the door where the voices were getting louder.

Logan felt miserable. "I haven't seen them since the day I turned eighteen." He started to tug Jess back down the hallway, but he was too late.

The door to his office flew open, a petite blonde stopping them in their tracks. "Logan James. We've been waiting here for almost an hour. They told us you'd be here right after lunch."

"What are you guys doing here?" Logan tried to keep his voice calm. He peeked at Jess sideways. She was intently studying his mother, who was wearing zebra print heels with a tight fitting white dress. Bright red-orange lipstick broke her monochromatic look. Great. This was the worst possible ending to their lunch date.

Logan's dad stepped out of the office behind his mother. He was dressed in his usual black Italian Brioni suit looking like he was on his way to a funeral.

"Dad." Logan nodded.

"Logan." He turned his steely gray eyes to Jess. He looked her up and down, his expression cold. "Who is this?"

CHAPTER NINE

JESS FELT LIKE a little girl again, stuck between two different worlds. Logan's dad seemed to graze her very skin with his look. She was used to people judging her by her skin color – she was either too light or too dark depending on who was criticizing her. But she could actually feel the hatred behind Mr. Jacob's eyes. Jess hadn't been this uncomfortable around anyone in a very long time. She looked over at Logan. His body was tense, his mouth drawn into a firm line.

Logan cleared his throat and stepped close to Jess. "This is Jess Platten. Jess these are my parents, Dave and Michelle Jacobs."

Jess was grateful for his closeness because she started feeling lightheaded. Both of his parents had turned their attention to her now, and she was frozen in place. She could only nod to them in greeting.

"What are you two doing here?" Logan directed this to his mother.

She pasted on a small smile and stepped back into Logan's office. His father followed her, his dress shoes clicking on the tile floor.

Logan leaned in to Jess and whispered, "I'm so sorry, Jess. I literally haven't seen them since I left home, and I have no idea why they are here now. I'll understand if you want to leave. They aren't very nice people."

Jess looked at his parents pacing in the small office. Even though they scared her, the journalist inside her felt there was more here to be learned. And the side of her that was attracted to Logan felt protective of him. In either case, she was not going to leave. She shook her head. "No, if I can survive lunch in the forgotten side of Seattle, I can handle your parents."

Logan hesitated as he looked at her, but then entered the office. Jess stepped in beside him.

His mother was running her finger over the pictures and awards on the bookshelf behind Logan's desk, and his father had commandeered Logan's chair. Jess decided to sit in one of the guest chairs in front of the desk. His father folded his hands on the desk in front of him and stared at her. Jess felt suddenly cold.

Logan walked over and stood beside Jess. "What are you doing here?" This was directed to his mother again.

Mr. Jacobs cleared his throat, and slowly looked away from Jess to focus on Logan. "We know you're graduating from this — place — soon and we have come to take you to home. You've proven your point, but now it's time to return to your duties."

"Is that so? And what duties would those be? The family business? Your business?" Logan crossed his arms and clenched his jaw. "I told you I wouldn't have anything to do with it. I'm not going back there. This is my home now."

Logan's dad stood up quickly, crashing the chair into the bookshelf behind him. Logan's mom had to sidestep in her high heels to quickly get out of the way.

"You will come home with us. Today. We have our jet on standby." He stepped around the desk and stood stiffly in front of Logan, his face contorted in anger.

Logan didn't back down. Instead, he stepped forward until he was standing just inches away from his dad. Logan was tall, but his dad still towered over him. Logan looked up and said, "You both need to leave now. I won't be going anywhere with you. I don't have any respect left for you or the family business."

His father's face clouded and he balled up his fists. "I will cut you out of everything if you do not come with us right now. I will not have any son of mine making meals like a servant and socializing with common people." He looked over at Jess, his anger smoldering visibly in his eyes. Jess saw where Logan got his ocean blue eyes, except there was nothing good behind his father's gaze.

Jess was up and out of her chair, her heart racing. Logan caught her around the waist before she could leave. He held her firmly to his side. She leaned into him and she could feel him shaking with rage.

"You both need to leave now." Logan said again, hardening his tone. He locked his attention on his father. His mother seemed to have lost some of her bravado and was hovering silently beside her husband.

No one moved or said anything. Jess thought for sure time had stopped, as the air slowly seemed to leave the room.

"Son, are you sure?" His mom's voice was pleading. She came close to Logan and put her hand on his arm. "We miss you at home." She looked sideways at her husband. "You belong with us."

Logan shook his head. "No, Mother. I belong here. I won't be going back." Logan leaned forward and kissed her on the forehead. "Goodbye, Mother."

She looked between Logan and her husband, her eyes filled with tears but her expression hard. She turned and walked out of the office, her heels clicking a fast tempo.

Jess watched as surprise passed over Mr. Jacobs's face. Without saying a word, he followed his wife out of the office. Jess felt her whole body relax as she watched them disappear down the hallway.

Without letting go of her, Logan turned face Jess. "I'm so sorry, Jess. That was the last thing I expected to happen today, and I'm sorry you had to witness that."

Jess pulled him closer so their faces were just inches apart. She tried to think of something to say as she looked into his brilliant blue eyes, but words just seemed insufficient. Instead, she leaned in and kissed him.

He returned the kiss, warm and confident, wrapping both his arms around her as she melted into him. She enjoyed his warm hands on her back and the way he smelled like cilantro and fresh limes. Realization struck that for once she wasn't afraid of being close to a man. She trusted him and felt safe.

Jess pulled back, breathless, and smiled up at him. "I don't know what just happened between you and your parents, but obviously you don't share their dislike of me."

He gave her a crooked smile. "It's that obvious?"

Jess's stomach fluttered as he leaned in for another kiss.

Finally, Logan let go of Jess. He looked slightly less shaken up from the confrontation. "How about if I explain about my parents as I show you around the university. That is if you're still up to it." He walked behind his desk and opened the top drawer to pull out a set of keys.

She smiled and nodded. Jess didn't care what they did as long as she was spending time with Logan. He took her hand and they headed back downstairs.

Jess wondered how parents could be that cold toward their own child. Logan's parents had treated him more like a bad business transaction rather than their own flesh and blood. Even though Jess's mom wasn't the most responsible, Jess always knew she was loved. Her mom was the only good thing in Nogales. Especially now that Jess could take care of herself.

CHAPTER TEN

LOGAN EXPLAINED THE layout of the building as they walked toward the kitchens. This helped him calm his emotions after seeing his parents. Why were they here now? They could've waited until after graduation to try to force him home. He hated how angry he still was at them.

Jess's closeness helped redirect his focus. He watched her facial expressions soften from fear and tension to curiosity as they walked around the building. How much should he tell her about his parents? Could he explain enough without revealing too many dark family secrets?

In the basement, the large commercial kitchens waited, dark and clean behind locked doors. Logan used his keys to unlock the closest kitchen and flipped on the lights.

From beside him, Jess gasped. "This is amazing," she said as she stepped into the room.

He smiled as he looked around the huge industrial kitchen. Stainless steel gleamed everywhere, from the large upright refrigerators and freezers lining the back wall, to the sturdy tables and large pots and pans that vied for space in between. The instructors were sticklers for cleanliness and it showed.

"Not exactly what I expected." Jess laughed. "I guess I thought it would look more like my home economics classroom in high school." She let go of his hand and walked along the row of tables.

"With as much money as we pay for an education here, I guess the school figures we need the very best to learn with." Logan loved being down here in the kitchens. This place had become like a second home to him over the last few years.

Dark hair cascaded in waves over her shoulders as she turned to regard him. "You seem happy here, in this space. Even after what happened upstairs. I thought you were unsure if you wanted to keep cooking."

Logan stopped beside a commercial mixer that was taller than he by several inches. Jess would see through him if he weren't honest, so he sighed and nodded. "Yes, I feel very much at home in the kitchens. It's confusing to me too. I enjoy the creation and experimental part of cooking. And the best part of the classes here is that we donate what we cook to the local Boys and Girls club. That's my favorite part." He smiled, remembering all the happy faces whenever he showed up with treats for the kids. "But when I have to cook the same thing over and over for the restaurant, it's just not the same feeling." He quickly added, "Although I love working at Enrique's. Just not forever."

Logan pulled out a stool and sat down. "And of course my parents still want me to go back to South Africa to start up a restaurant. I know I don't want to do that, but I haven't figured out what else to do. If I could just stay here at the university and cook for the kids I'd be happy." He gave her a weak smile.

"So you'd rather cook for an after-school program than make a ton of money at an upscale restaurant?" Jess pulled up a stool next to him.

Logan nodded. "So far, it's the only thing here I've found that I enjoy. Before I came to America, I lived for a summer in a small village where I learned to cook. They taught me how to cook for many people, and how to use spices and herbs freshly harvested from the gardens. I learned to love cooking. But my parents hated everything about it, and eventually found a way to make it so I couldn't stay there any longer." He looked away from Jess, emotions threatening to overwhelm him. "So I moved to America the day after I turned eighteen."

"How did your parents make it so you couldn't stay there any longer? It sounds like you learned a lot there." Jess put her hand on his arm, warming him with her touch.

Logan turned back only to get caught up in her deep brown eyes. She had shared so much with him. If he wanted this to work between them, he'd need to trust her fully. He nodded slightly to himself as he made the decision to open up to her. "I didn't exactly go to live in that village with my parents' permission. About six months before my eighteenth birthday, I decided I couldn't live with them anymore. I detested how horribly they treated people and how they used others to get rich. One night I took one of their cars and drove out of the city until I ran out of gas. The villagers where I broke down took pity on me and let me stay. They were very kind to me, and I finally felt what it was like to be loved and accepted. My parents didn't care that I had left on my own, or that I had taken their car – they were just angry I was trying to leave the family business. To punish me, my parents found ways to destroy the villagers' way of life. The local officials wouldn't even do anything to help against my parents." Logan felt the nightmare trying to reach inside him again.

Jess put her hand on his arm. "That's horrible, Logan. I'm so sorry you had to go through that." She leaned into him. "How were they able to hurt an entire community?"

"My family owns many restaurants, diamond mines, financial institutions, farms, and they also control most of the transportation in the area. Deliveries of food, water filters, household goods, and medicines ceased to make it to us. I ended up returning home so my parents would leave the villagers alone."

Jess moved her hand down his arm to clasp his hand again. "If I hadn't seen so many people hurt each other in my line of work, I would wonder how your parents could ever do such horrible things. I don't ask that anymore. But why would they be here now after not seeing you since you left?"

Logan's instinct was to start pacing again, but Jess held tight to his hand. He wanted to trust that she was asking these questions because she cared about him, not because she was chasing after a news story. "I'm turning twenty-five in a couple of weeks. My grandfather left a sizable trust for me. I have no siblings, so I'm the only heir. His only conditions were that I needed to be twenty-five to receive it, and I had to invest half of it back into the business within a year." Logan shrugged his shoulders. "I'm sure you can understand now why I don't want any more money to go back into their business. By showing up here unannounced at my school, I think they want to make sure I return to South Africa and claim my inheritance."

"That's a lot of pressure to put on you. I understand now why your parents weren't so thrilled to see me with you." She looked down at their entwined hands, light and dark. "Because of the color of my skin."

Logan was surprised she stated it as a matter of fact. She wasn't angry or bitter. He nodded and opened his mouth to apologize for them again, but she stopped him with a kiss. He returned the kiss, relieved she wasn't upset with his troubled confession. He opened up his arms, and she sank into him. They fit perfectly. He moved one hand to the back of her head and dug his fingers into her thick hair. He'd been wanting to do that since they shared lunch. Their kisses grew deeper and more urgent as he enjoyed her warm body pressed up to his. Logan wished they were somewhere more private. He couldn't remember if there were more classes in the kitchens tonight, but he hoped they wouldn't be interrupted. Although there were many women at the university who had asked him out, he had never felt anything like the connection he had with Jess. He couldn't get enough of her, and despite his parents putting a damper on the afternoon; it was turning out very enjoyable after all.

CHAPTER ELEVEN

JESS WAS TOTALLY lost in Logan's kisses and the feel of his warm body against hers. She had never felt so safe or worthy of this kind of passion. Such things usually came with a price.

She tugged the back of his shirt out of his pants so she could run her hands up his smooth muscular back. His breath caught, and Jess smiled as he reacted to her touch. She moved her hands lower and started to trace the waist of his pants toward the front, when the sound of a door slamming sounded from the hallway.

They both pulled back, breathless. Jess looked over at the door. When she looked back at Logan he had a huge grin on his face.

"The janitor. We'd better get going before he makes it to this room." His face was flushed, and Jess was certain hers was too. Logan disentangled himself from her and tucked in his shirt.

Jess couldn't keep from smiling either. Every move he made was enticing. She had to look away so she could get her heart rate under control.

She was disappointed they'd been interrupted, but she knew it was probably better that they stopped when they had. They'd just met yesterday, and she had never gone this far with any man so quickly. The few relationships she'd had tended to be longterm and not as exciting as this. Besides, she reminded herself, she was here as a visitor in this city. She wasn't staying.

And most importantly, this man was way out of her league. He had every head turning here on campus.

"Ready?" Logan held out his hand to her. They heard another door slam, closer.

"Where to now?" She smiled and took his hand.

He drew her to him and gave her another kiss. "You're really willing to trust me with more of your time after this day?"

The last few minutes weren't too bad." Not bad at all, she thought as she kissed him back.

Laughing, he pulled her toward the door. As Logan locked the classroom back up and then nodded to the janitor as they passed him, Jess felt like a schoolgirl sneaking out as they hurried down the hallway.

They toured the rest of the university hand in hand. There were several classroom buildings, one tall dorm and one parking structure. The auditorium and administration building rounded out the rest of the university's property. Although Jess tried to pay attention to what he was saying, all she could think of was their kisses in the kitchen, and how much she wanted more.

Jess turned around in a circle to take in all the buildings and landscape and students rushing around them. It was a beautiful campus. In the distance, she saw the Space Needle standing tall over the city. Seemed no matter where she went here, she always saw the Space Needle. She could really get used to this city.

As several students hurried past them, Jess stopped in her tracks and looked at Logan. "I totally forgot to be looking out for my story." She frowned and felt her body go numb as she realized she had let her emotions get in the way of her goal. The young singer could've walked right past her, and she wouldn't have noticed. She was too caught up in Logan and the chemistry between them.

"Your story. I'm so sorry, I forgot too." He motioned to the Admin building behind them. "And the office is closed until tomorrow."

"I only have another week here, I really needed that story. Do you really think the office would know which student here she's visiting? They wouldn't keep track of that, would they?"

Logan shrugged. "Not officially, no. But it's a relatively small school. Not too much can go on here without someone knowing."

The sun was setting, coloring the sky in pastel colors. Jess looked through the trees growing between the buildings. It was beautiful and served as a reminder of the new life she was trying to create. She took a deep breath and turned back to Logan. "You're right. I'm sorry I got so worked up. It can wait one more day." She smiled and looped her arm through his, pulling him close.

"Well then, the least I can do is cook for you. I think its only fair after what I've put you through." Logan kissed her on the forehead and pulled her toward the dorms.

"Really? The great chef Logan is going to cook for me? Dinner for just the two of us?"

"Only if we don't have any more uninvited guests." He grinned down at her.

Jess untangled her arm from his and playfully pushed him. "Are there any more upset family members I need to know about?"

He caught his balance and laughed. "Honestly, we should be safe. When my parents say they're leaving, they do. Leaving is one thing they're really good at. And they're the only family I have that would be trying to track me down."

"I'm just sorry my presence made it worse between you and your parents." Jess smiled at him weakly.

Logan caught her up in his arms. "None of that was your fault. Okay? It had nothing to do with you, the problem is all theirs." His eyes were intense, and Jess could tell he meant it. She nodded and he kissed her on the mouth, drawing their bodies even closer.

After a few minutes of kissing, Jess smiled up at him. "So do you have a roommate?" She cringed. "I didn't mean for that to sound so forward."

Chuckling, he let her go just far enough to hold her hand. He led them to the ten-story dorm building. "I have my own room. They call these dorm rooms, but they're actually small apartments. Can't have culinary students cooking ramen noodles on a hot plate."

She was taken aback when he let her into his apartment. His place was not only clean, but also tastefully decorated. There was a modern black couch and chair, stylish rugs and end tables. The kitchen was immaculate, with gleaming pots and pans hanging from a metal frame in the ceiling. Several small appliances sat waiting on the counters.

"I was not expecting this."

"What, you expected wicker furniture and pizza boxes?" Logan feigned offense.

"Well, yes, honestly." Jess walked past a side table with mail, keys, and pictures efficiently organized. "Did you do this all by yourself?"

He nodded and headed toward the kitchen. "You saw how well my parents were dressed. They raised me to know the finer aspects of having loads of money." He opened the sparkling stainless steel refrigerator and started pulling out food. "My uncle, however, taught me how to conserve my money and how to find the best deals. So when I moved here, I scoured the used furniture and appliance stores."

Jess sat down at one of the bar stools at the kitchen island to watch Logan. "I'm impressed. A man of many talents. I'm surprised no one has snatched you up to force a ring on your finger."

The cutting board he pulled out landed on the counter with a soft thud, and then he began cutting the vegetables that immediately went into a pan on the stove. "Nope. No marriage for me. All the women I knew in South Africa were only after my money." He looked up at Jess. "My parents had a way of making sure to set me up with royalty or women whose families would benefit their businesses."

"But what about here in America? You don't live rich, and from what I saw in the bar, most of those women were after you for your status as a judge. They don't know who you really are, or how much your family is worth?" Jess watched as he expertly cut and diced different vegetables with ease.

"My family is only well known in South Africa. That's part of why I moved here. To escape their name as well as their business reputation." He shrugged.

"Couldn't you have just moved to a different area or country down there? A big city, maybe? So they couldn't harm the people there?"

"Are you allergic to seafood?" He held up a package of shrimp.

Jess shook her head and waited for him to answer her question while he prepared the shrimp and add it to the vegetables. Only after he put the lid on the pot, did he turn back to face her.

CHAPTER TWELVE

LOGAN LOVED SEEING Jess sitting in his kitchen. "After the day we just had, do you mind if we don't talk anymore about my parents?" He walked around the island to stand in front of her.

She swiveled on the stool to face him. "I'm sure we could find other topics." She pulled him toward her and kissed him. She then wrapped her legs around his waist, making his heart rate spike. He moved his arms around her and deepened their kiss, his desire overriding his earlier caution.

Over the sound of his heart beating loudly in his ears, Logan heard the sizzle of the food on the stove. He drew back from the kiss and whispered, "I need to rescue the food before it burns."

She released him, grinning. "I know how it feels." She touched her swollen lips. Her face flushed when she looked up at him.

He didn't want to stop, but he couldn't ruin the first meal he cooked for her. He walked around the counter island and stirred the shrimp and vegetables. He counted to ten, calming his heart rate before looking up at her again.

She was watching him intently, her green eyes taking his breath away. He smiled back at her as she blushed again. "You're very beautiful, especially when you blush."

"Well, you're very addicting." Her blush deepened.

Logan's heart skipped a beat. She had no idea how she affected him. "It's hard to believe we've only known each other a few days." He pulled down two plates and added stir-fry to each one. "As you guessed last night, I'm not usually so comfortable with people like I am with you." Logan's stomach twisted as he realized how true that was.

"I feel the same way. Kind of crazy, huh?" She smiled. He was sure that smile was going to be his undoing.

While they ate, Logan learned that Jess liked the same sci-fi and action movies he did and that she loved reading. What more could he want in a woman?

Jess helped him clean up the kitchen after they finished eating. Then he went through his frozen cache of pre-made desserts that he kept on hand and pulled out a wedge of cheesecake large enough to split. A drizzle of homemade hot fudge completed each slice. Smiling with anticipation, he slipped one of the slices on front of Jess than say across from her and watched as she took the first bite.

Her eyes sparkled as she smiled at him. "This is delicious. Did you make this too?" Jess asked as she licked her spoon clean.

Relieved that she liked it, Logan picked up his fork to eat his slice. "Yes, this was last week's assignment. I made a full cheesecake, and then froze portions to bring home." He smiled. "I'm glad you like it. It's a recipe I created myself. It's a little different than your normal cheesecake."

"Really? It's amazing." She put another bite into her mouth.

Logan chuckled. "I've often thought of making my own cookbook."

"Why haven't you? This is really good."

Logan shrugged. "I have a collection of all the recipes I've created, but I wouldn't know the first step in actually publishing one."

Jess got up and rinsed her dish off. She turned around and leaned against the counter. "I'm sure it wouldn't take a lot of research to figure out how to put one together. I bet it would be a lot like writing a media story, where you need different experts to edit it and help get it out to the world." Her gaze unfocused for a few seconds before landing back on Logan. Her expression was sad. "That reminds me that I need to start out early tomorrow to track down another story. I don't have much time left here in Seattle. I should be going back to the hotel."

Logan got up and walked over to her. "Do you have to leave so soon?" His voice was husky as he looked into her eyes. He didn't want her to leave. "We shouldn't have any more interruptions."

Jess laughed softly. "That's what I'm afraid of." She placed her hands on either side of his face and kissed him deeply.

Before Logan could respond, she squirmed away and stepped out of the kitchen. "I'm very attracted to you, Logan, and I don't trust myself around you."

Logan stepped closer, his heart sinking. "You think we're going too fast?"

She nodded and gave him a quick kiss on the lips. "Probably. And we both have major projects in our lives that we need to concentrate on this week. As much as I would love to just stay here with you," she kissed him again, "I think we need to focus on achieving our immediate goals first, and then we'll see where we are afterward." Logan saw a touch of sadness behind her smile.

He got her jacket for her and helped her into it. "I understand, Jess. But I think we can do both. We don't have to choose between our careers and getting to know each other. We can do this together."

Jess shook her head slowly. "I don't think I can do both. When I'm writing a story, it consumes me. I've never been very good at balancing my life."

"I could help you find your story. I'm sure someone on campus saw her." Logan hated how desperate he sounded. He somehow felt if she walked out now, he wouldn't see her again.

Jess pulled her jacket tighter around her. "I think I need to do this on my own. I'm really sorry." She looked down.

Logan lifted her chin, forcing her to meet his gaze. "You know where to find me." He kissed her and wrapped her in a tight embrace. She melted into him, shaking.

When she pulled back, Logan could see she was on the verge of tears. She turned and hurried out the door. Logan stood there, stunned. He closed his eyes, memorizing their kiss, her scent, and the feel of her in his arms.

That night Logan didn't sleep well. The day had been a roller coaster of emotions. Even with his parents' visit, all he could think of was Jess, and he drove himself crazy trying to figure out what he'd done wrong and how he could fix it. Had he missed something? Had he pushed too hard? He had finally let his guard down and gotten to know someone. If he'd met Jess after her big story was finished, would tonight have turned out differently? Maybe if his parents hadn't shown up Jess might not have been so freaked out. Anger toward his parents rose familiar in his chest as he again relived the incident in his office that afternoon.

Finally, too unsettled for sleep, Logan threw off his covers and paced his bedroom.

Running his hand through his hair, he checked the bedside clock. He had three hours before he had to report to his job. Might as well get ready for work since he couldn't sleep. Mechanically, he went through the routine of showering and getting dressed. Then he grabbed his keys and headed out the door. He would walk to work since he was so early. The cool night air would keep him awake. And it would give him some more time to think about what to do about Jess, if anything.

CHAPTER THIRTEEN

JESS WASHED HER face quickly and put on her leggings and a nightshirt. She pulled back the covers to her bed, but didn't get in. There was no way she was going to get sleep after this day.

And now this revelation about Logan's past both intrigued her and made her stomach churn. He had told her in confidence about his family's immoral business affairs. She knew he'd been conflicted about telling her. She had seen it in his eyes.

As bad as the story he told was, Jess knew there was something more he wasn't telling her. She walked over to the small desk beside her bed, opened her laptop, and settled into the chair.

After a few hours of research, Jess's eyes were burning, and she was forced to turn her laptop off. Her mind was still running in circles when she flopped down on the bed to attempt sleep.

The sun woke her up a few hours later as it streamed through the hastily closed curtains and fell across her face.

She sat up and pushed her unruly hair out of her face. She looked over at her laptop and all the pages of notes strung out across the desk and groaned.

The information she had dug up last night was truly a career-changing news story. Logan had been right to not tell her the whole story. It was horrible, and her heart ached for him. What his parents had done was absolutely inhuman, and the fact that they had gotten away with it all these years made her blood boil. If she were able to bring this story to her editor and expose what had happened in that little village Logan loved so much, Jess could choose any journalism job she wanted. And maybe bring some justice to those innocent people.

Jess shook her head and got up from the bed. If she wrote this story, it would hurt Logan and any future they might have had together. He would hate her, and he would have every right to. This story would tear his family apart, and would ruin his reputation in the process. A reputation he was trying hard to build separate from his family's affairs. Wasn't this exactly what she had promised herself she wouldn't do?

Yet, this kind of international human-interest story was exactly what Jess needed to break in to the serious side of journalism. She could get away from the gossip columns and move on from her past.

Jess stepped into the shower and leaned her head against the cool tile, letting the hot water massage her back. Would it be worth earning success if she ruined Logan's family life and career? The dilemma gave her a headache and she stayed under the hot water until it ran cold.

She quickly got dressed, grabbed her laptop and notes, and headed downstairs. Jess took the back stairs and out the delivery entrance to avoid the possibility of running into Logan. He had tried calling twice, which she had ignored. Right now, he thought she just needed time to work on her story. He didn't know yet that what she was really researching was his story. Jess shoved that thought to the back of her mind. She still had more research to do before she would decide whether or not to keep pursuing this story.

There was a chill in the air, and Jess pulled her light jacket tighter around her. Autumn was on its way in the big city, but at least it wasn't raining.

A few blocks away from the hotel Jess flagged a taxi to take her to the university. Her head still throbbed so she was in no mood to walk. She needed to get some caffeine. She smiled to herself. She knew that would be easy to find, since she was in the city of espresso. Seattle was called the Emerald City, but everyone knew that you came here for great coffee.

The streets grew familiar and soon the taxi deposited her in front of the same building where she stood with Logan just last night. Her heart constricted as she remembered the heat that sparked so quickly between them.

She took a few breaths and walked toward the admin building. This time she made sure to pay attention to the faces passing her. There was still a small glimpse of hope that she could find that girl again and then she could write her original story.

She hurried past the dorm building and kept her head down. She was pretty sure Logan had to work this morning, but she still didn't want to run into him yet. She would work both stories until she could be sure of one of them. She had to turn something in to her editor.

Inside the admin building she looked for signs to the registrar. She would start there since they usually knew all the students.

She found the right office and waited in a small line, until a perky blonde called her over.

"Good morning! What can I help you with today?" Well, this girl had already had too much caffeine this morning.

"I'm hoping you can help me find my friend. I'm visiting in town and I dropped my phone yesterday and lost all my contacts. I was supposed to meet up with her somewhere near campus for dinner tonight."

The blonde's smile dropped. "I can't give out personal information of our students."

Jess smiled and leaned over the counter. "I understand, really I do. My friend isn't actually a student here. She's just dating one." Jess looked at the wall next to the girl where there was a bulletin board with flyers, one of them advertising the cooking competition. She nodded her head in that direction. "My friend's boyfriend is in that competition. Isn't that exciting?" It was hard pretending to be chipper without coffee in her system.

The girl looked over at the flyer and then back to Jess. Her bright white smile was back. "Yes, that's the highlight of the year here on campus. Which one is your friend's boyfriend?"

Jess looked back at the poster and studied the nine faces with their names below each picture. She picked the most handsome one, and hoped he wasn't already taken. "That's him! She sent me pictures of him." Jess held her breath while waiting to see if the girl would take the bait, or if she had completely struck out.

The blonde bounced up and down on the balls of her feet. She had probably been a cheerleader in high school. "Oh! That's Derek. He's the favorite around here to win this year." She frowned. "I haven't heard that he has a girlfriend though." She narrowed her eyes at Jess. "Every girl on campus has tried to get his attention. I would known if he had a girlfriend."

Great, Jess thought. Sounds like this girl has been practically stalking this guy. Jess met her gaze. "My friend did say he wouldn't actually commit to her. She's just hopeful. And besides she's a celebrity of sorts, so they would have to keep their relationship kind of quiet." Jess shrugged and smiled sadly. "Sounds like she has some competition here. No wonder she wanted me to visit. Now I really need to find her."

Jess pushed away from the counter. As she turned away, the blonde spoke up. "Wait! Your friend might be at one of the practices they hold every afternoon down in the kitchens." She looked over at the poster again. "I know Derek has been at every practice session. He's determined to win." She looked back at Jess and leaned forward, her cleavage almost falling out of her tight t-shirt. "You might want to encourage your friend to leave him alone until after the competition. You know, so he can concentrate." She gave Jess a stiff smile and stood up straight again.

Jess matched the blonde's fake smile. "Thanks, I'll be sure to let her know."

Jess forced herself to walk out of the building, biting the inside of her cheek. She had to have lost a few brain cells from talking to that vacuous girl, but at least she had a lead on her story.

Jess paused outside the culinary building. Of course, the same place she needed to look for Derek was the very same place she might run into Logan. Maybe since Logan was a judge this time, he wouldn't be at any of the practice sessions. Jess pushed through the doors. There were a lot more students in the hall during the day than there was last night with Logan.

Jess walked down the hallway until she encountered a group of students that were standing around a bulletin board. Jess stretched to look over several of their heads. It was a schedule of practice times and the rooms the students in the competition would need to report to.

Excited, Jess pushed to the front to find Derek's name. When she found it, her heart sunk. His time slot wasn't for another couple of hours. Since she didn't know where he lived, she would have to wait until his time in the kitchens.

Jess made her way out of the crowd and walked back outside into the sunshine. She headed for the main building. They would have Wi-Fi there so she could at least continue her online research.

Jess found a fairly large study area, complete with a coffee shop, snacks, printers, and of course free Wi-Fi. Then she settled down in a corner where she could spread her notes out. There wasn't too much more she could do to find her original story at the moment, so she would see what she could track down on Logan's family.

CHAPTER FOURTEEN

WORK SEEMED TO go slower than usual. Logan had practically drunk an entire pot of coffee trying to stay awake. It was right before the lunchtime rush, so at least he had plenty to do. Enrique was a wonderful boss, but Logan was bored with prepping the same food every morning for the same recipes. Not having slept at all last night didn't help. Between being mentally stagnant and physically tired, Logan was ready to curl up and take a nap under the sink.

His shift finally over, he took a taxi back to his dorm. After a quick shower to get the onion smell off and to wake him up a bit, he headed back down the elevator. The only thing that was driving him now, allowing him to push through the boredom of all the monotonous cooking at work and school, was his side project of new recipes, and the preparations for the competition next week.

Logan headed to the culinary building and back down to the kitchens. It would be a few hours before the competition students would be coming down here for their practice times. Logan went to the same kitchen he had taken Jess to the night before. He smiled as he entered the room, remembering their kisses. He wondered what might've happened if the janitor hadn't interrupted them. His body warmed at the thought.

Logan walked over to a bay of lockers and dialed the combination on his lock. It took him three tries to get it right. He shook his head. Maybe Jess was right. Maybe now wasn't the right time for them — they were too distracted by each other.

He finally got it open, pulled out his notebooks, and spread them out on the nearest counter. Most of them had loose pieces of paper that were already scrawled on. Logan tried to organize them, make some sense of them. These were his own recipes that he hoped to make into a cookbook someday.

He finally got the papers wrangled into some sort of order and placed safely back inside the notebooks. Just that little bit of work seemed to drain the energy out of him. He needed some coffee if he was going to try out his newest flan recipe later. He could take over a corner of the kitchen while the others practiced for the competition. But first, he needed caffeine.

He gathered his notebooks up and headed to the commons. A good strong cup of coffee would help him wake up so he could concentrate on something other than falling asleep or kissing Jess.

Several students stopped him on the way to the commons. He made small talk with them and then hurried on. If he didn't get some caffeine soon he'd be sleep walking.

Once in the commons he headed for the coffee shop. He was forced to make more small talk while he waited in line. As soon as he had his coffee in hand, he made a beeline for the back sitting area.

Logan came around a corner and stopped, his coffee threatening to spill over. There in the corner where he usually retreated to, was Jess. She hadn't noticed him yet, her concentration on piles of papers surrounding her laptop.

Logan's heart pounded. Her lips were drawn tight in concentration, her gorgeous brown eyes intent on the paper in front of her. Jess had said she needed space to work on her project. Had she found the girl she was looking for here? Logan wasn't sure if the sheer amount of printouts around Jess was a good sign or not.

He hesitated only a few seconds more before walking over. She was the reason he was so tired today, and he couldn't get his mind off her. He would just see how she was doing, he justified.

Logan stepped right next to her table and still she didn't notice him. He looked around at the paperwork. News printouts and pages of hand written notes surrounded her.

His skin grew cold, and he couldn't breathe as he skimmed over some of the words. Most of the printouts scattered around Jess had his family's name on them, and pictures of what happened to his friends.

"Oh my goodness, Logan. I didn't see you come over."

He watched mutely, lost for words, as she scrambled to gather up all the papers.

She looked down at the pile of paper in her hands. "This isn't what it looks like."

Logan clenched his hands, almost dropping his notebooks and coffee. He struggled to keep his voice low. "I thought you needed time to find that girl and to work on that article. Not to do this." He motioned with his arm at the loose papers she hadn't gathered up yet.

He could see pleading in Jess's eyes, but he couldn't tell her it was all right because it wasn't. "I was, I am. I'm just waiting for Derek's practice time in the kitchens. He's the singer's type. She might come to watch him cook." Her eyes welled up with tears, and she clung to the papers in her arms. "This is just my curiosity. I wasn't really planning on doing anything with this." She dropped the papers into her lap and lowered her head into her hands.

"If you didn't intend to use the story, then why all this research?" Why couldn't he have just cut it off after their lunch?

"I'm sorry. I really am." Jess gathered up the papers again and stuffed them into her backpack. When she had cleaned it all up and put away her laptop, she stood up to face Logan.

Logan hadn't moved. He couldn't move – he was frozen in place with anger, fear, and betrayal. He wasn't sure what to say or do. This woman could ruin his entire life with the information she had in front of her. He had made the decision to open his heart to Jess. He had known what the consequences were, and now he was facing the worst. He was angry with her, but he was furious at himself.

She stood there, Logan blocking her only escape. He wasn't going to move or make anything easy for her. "We've only known each other a couple of days, so I know I don't really have any right to ask you not to run that story. I made a decision to share that information with you."

She looked up at him, her expression breaking his heart.

Logan swallowed hard and continued, "I thought there was something between us. I guess I was wrong." He pivoted out of her way, just enough to let her squeeze by.

"I'm not really sure what I'm doing yet, Logan. Really." Logan couldn't look at her. She lifted her hand and placed it lightly on his arm. He didn't move, although he felt her touch as if it were burning him. "There was something there between us. I told you I couldn't do work and social stuff at the same time." Her voice was barely a whisper. Then she turned and hurried out of the commons leaving Logan standing by himself, shaking with emotion.

He stood there a moment longer before he strode out as well. He imagined he could feel everyone's eyes on him as he left.

He saw Jess head toward the culinary building, so he turned and headed toward his dorm. He threw the untouched coffee in the trash outside his building and headed up the elevator.

He slammed his door closed and threw the recipe notebooks on the counter. Not caring about the mess he left behind, Logan stripped off his clothes, leaving a trail from the kitchen to his bedroom. He flopped onto the bed worn out physically and emotionally. Right before he fell asleep he remembered Jess saying that she thought there was something between them. In his exhaustion, his subconscious grabbed onto that hopeful comment and allowed him to fall asleep.

CHAPTER FIFTEEN

JESS REACHED THE culinary building and stepped inside with a heavy heart. She leaned against the wall to steady herself. Why had she allowed herself to get to know Logan? She had known she wasn't ready. She needed to concentrate on her career first. Didn't she? She pushed off from the wall and went in search of a bathroom.

As she passed by the kitchen where she was with Jess last night she peeked in and saw a few people clanking bowls and pans around. Hopefully Derek was one of them.

Jess found the restroom at the end of the hallway. She placed her backpack down and splashed water on her face. Maybe if the girl came tonight she could still write her original story. Then she could apologize to Logan and they could start over.

Jess shook her head at her reflection. What was she kidding? Even if she could pull off the celebrity story, which was a big if, Logan had no reason to forgive her. They hadn't known each other long enough for him to want to deal with any of her issues. And she knew she had broken his trust. She sighed and straightened up. She grabbed her backpack and pushed hard on the door to leave. There was a muffled yell after the door hit something solid.

Jess peeked around the partly opened door and came face to face with the pretty blonde from the Admin building. She was sitting on the ground rubbing her head.

Suppressing a giggle, Jess reached down to help the girl up. "I'm really sorry. I shouldn't have pushed it open so hard. Are you all right?"

The blonde looked up and a flash of recognition flitted across her perfect face. A face that now had an additional red spot growing on her forehead. "You. I see you found the right place." She allowed Jess to help her up, but looked like she wanted to strangle her.

Jess nodded as she thought of all the ways this girl could blow her story. "Ummm, yes. I haven't seen my friend yet, though." With a tight smile, Jess turned and walked quickly down the hallway before the blonde could say anything further.

She paused at the door of the kitchen and scanned the room for Logan. Although she should've been relieved when she didn't see him there, she felt a bit disappointed. She slipped in and found a place along the wall where other students stood watching the cooks in the middle of the room.

Derek was working at the table where Logan had kissed her last night. Jess's hand automatically went to her lips, remembering the scent and feel of him touching her. She inwardly groaned.

Focus! She stood up straight and tried to concentrate on the crowd around her. She needed to finish this story before she got more sidetracked.

The blonde had stepped into the room and went to stand on the far side. That was fine with Jess — she didn't want to have to answer any nosy questions.

By the time the chefs all had their food mixed and into the ovens, Jess felt sick to her stomach. The girl wasn't here. And Derek was flirting with several other girls, just like the blonde had warned her. If Derek wasn't the singer's type, then who was? Everything she had learned about this girl pointed to her dating someone here on campus. Maybe her injuries had been severe enough to send her back home.

Jess made her way to the door, sickened at the realization that she had probably lost this story. Once out of the building, she put her backpack on and kept walking. She needed to think, and walking was her favorite way of clearing her head and getting her creative ideas flowing.

As she rounded the campus, Jess talked herself off the ledge of despair. She couldn't give up now. There was always the cooking competition. She needed to make sure she had a seat in the audience that night. She would go back to the university tomorrow and find the schedule. Logan said it was next week sometime.

She picked up the pace as she thought about Logan. Why couldn't she just get him out of her head? It had just been lunch and dinner and a few kisses. Yes, they seemed to connect very quickly with one another, and they had felt comfortable enough to share very private information with each other. But he really hadn't told her everything, right? Her pace slowed down. Yes, that was right. Logan was upset because he had told her his secrets, but he really hadn't. He had only told her a small piece of the puzzle. She'd figured out the rest on her own. She mentally kicked herself. She should've brought that point up at the coffee shop instead of being tongue-tied and running out of there like an emotional wreck.

Jess looked up and saw that she was almost to her hotel. Should she call Logan and talk to him about this? Should she ask why he had hidden such a huge secret from her if he supposedly had so many feelings for her? Confusion settled over her like a dark storm cloud.

Once up in her room, she unloaded her laptop and all the notes. Then she threw herself across the bed and stared up at the ceiling. She only had one more week to do what she had come here for – get the story of a lifetime. She had thrown all her savings at this chance. There was no way she was going back without a story that would get her noticed. She enjoyed being so far from her past, and far away from the fear that dominated her life.

She rolled over onto her belly and looked over at her computer sitting on the desk next to the bed. All of her research lay scattered around, bits and pieces of Logan's past. His family secrets printed off the Internet, staring at her in black and white. Jess shook her head and got up off the bed. She walked over to the papers and shuffled idly through them.

This was exactly what he had been afraid of, Jess chided herself. He'd come all the way to the United States to get away from his past. Just like she had traveled north to get away from hers. His wasn't a physical fear like hers was, but it was just as debilitating. His was a fear of being part of a family that could do such horrible things. Jess stared at the pictures in her hands. Black faces laying in rows, sheets barely covering their bodies. Men, women, children, all dead because of Logan's parents. They had to have used considerable influence to stay out of jail for such atrocities.

Anger surged within Jess. She grabbed all the paper off the desk and ripped it into little pieces. She then crammed it all into the wastebasket. There was no way she was going to bring Logan's fears to light. Or put the survivors through more pain and torment. They deserved better, and so did Logan.

Besides, how long since she'd felt this safe with someone? She wasn't afraid of Logan's touches – in fact she welcomed them. She thought of his hands touching her and him kissing her all the time. She had to try to fix things between them.

Exhilarated at her decision, Jess tried calling Logan. She would tell him she wasn't going to pursue his story. That she would figure something else out. Would he forgive her?

Logan didn't answer. She left a message. What if it was too late? What if he couldn't get over the fact that she had been willing to expose his secrets? How could he ever trust her again?

Jess sat down hard on the bed. And what about her other problem — that of not having a story to turn in to her editor? What would she do once the week was over and she didn't have any more money for a hotel? She didn't even have a plane ticket back home, not that she wanted to go back there. She had edged all her bets on this story.

Jess slipped off her shoes and slipped under the covers. Maybe tomorrow she could try to find Logan and apologize. It took a long time for her to fall asleep as she replayed different scenarios between her and Logan in her head. The good ones ended in kissing. The bad woke her up. She grasped onto the good visions and finally fell asleep.

CHAPTER SIXTEEN

LOGAN'S ALARM WENT off, and it felt like he had hardly slept at all. This was becoming a bad habit. He couldn't get Jess off his mind and he spent most of the night trying to think of anything but her. He had failed miserably and ended up dreaming about their fight in the coffee shop.

Grouchy and tired, Logan padded into the bathroom and stood under the hot shower. He then grabbed his work clothes and finished getting dressed in the kitchen while eating cold leftovers.

His mind kept going back to what Jess had been looking at. His family's secret. The horrible things they had done to his friends.

He finished tying his shoes and headed out the door. At five in the morning, it was still pitch dark. His ride was already waiting for him, his usual cabbie idling at the curb. He had decided to call him instead of walking to work today.

"Good morning, Ernie." Logan yawned as he plopped down in the back seat.

"Looks like you didn't sleep much, Mr. J."

Logan shook his head. "I slept, just not well. I'm going to need a lot of caffeine to get through my shift today."

Ernie's head bobbed up and down. "Getting off at the usual time? Need a ride home?"

Logan ran his hand down his face. "Yes, I think I'll definitely need a ride today. With the competition getting closer, I need to make sure all the details are getting taken care of."

"Sure thing. The competition is next week?"

"Yep, less than a week away."

"Good, I always get lots of extra fares from the hotel during the competitions." Ernie grinned in the rear view mirror at Logan.

Logan leaned his head against the window, hoping the cold glass would wake him up. He hated to think of what kind of morning he was going to have being this tired and working with knives.

Ernie dropped him off in the alleyway behind Enrique's. Logan pushed through the back door, knowing the cooks would already be there pulling vegetables for him to start prepping. Logan diverted to the coffee pot in the employee break room and helped himself to a large cup of straight black coffee.

Logan kept a steady stream of coffee in his system while he worked his shift. Although he still had a hard time keeping Jess off his mind, the time went fast and soon it was noon and time to clean up to leave.

He wandered out to the front to let Enrique know he was leaving. Enrique could always be found wandering from table to table talking with the customers. They loved him. He was outgoing and passionate about his food and his restaurant. He knew all of his regulars by name.

Although Logan loved to cook, he couldn't see himself doing something like this forever. He knew he could never be as personable and patient with people like Enrique.

Enrique noticed Logan standing by the kitchen door and steered his way through the tables.

"Heading home, Logan?" Enrique's eyes sparkled. He lived for this place and it energized him.

"Back to the university to work on competition details. You know how that goes." Logan worked up a weary smile for his boss.

"Yes, always lots of work. Don't forget to grab the posters." Enrique clapped Logan on the shoulder.

Logan smiled. "I won't. I'll grab them right now." Enrique always sponsored the cooking competition every year, so Logan would hang posters advertising the restaurant all over the university.

One of the hostesses caught Enrique's attention just then, so Logan took the opportunity to slip back through the kitchen. He grabbed the stack of posters as he headed out the back door. These posters were advertisement for Enrique's upcoming Cinco De Mayo celebration. It was very popular among the college crowd.

Ernie was waiting for him with a fresh cup of coffee.

On the way to the university, Logan checked his phone. There was a message from Jess. After trying to reach her and not getting any answer, now she was finally calling him back? Did he want to deal with this right now? He remembered the hurt look on her face yesterday at the coffee shop, and his own anger that had boiled over. He shouldn't care. He was the one injured here.

He pushed play on the voicemail before he could change his mind. He closed his eyes and took a deep breath. She wanted to meet up with him and talk about yesterday. Her voice made him want to go to her and gather her up in his arms and kiss her. How could he miss someone after only knowing her a few days?

He opened his eyes and squinted at the buildings as they drove past. He needed to stop thinking about her. He had this last competition to get through, and then he needed to figure out what he was going to do next. He had enough to worry about. Besides, she was the one who had said they needed to concentrate on their careers first.

He was, however, curious what she wanted to talk about. Had she already finished writing the story on his family? Did she just need more information from him? Was he going to be in her article?

Good grief, Logan. You just need to stay away from her. He pocketed his phone and forced himself to think of what he needed to do the rest of the day.

"Mr. J?" Ernie looked concerned.

"I'm sorry, Ernie. What were you saying?" Logan didn't remember hearing anything Ernie was talking about. He forced himself to sit up straight and concentrate.

"I was just saying there was a very pretty woman asking about you this morning. You have an admirer, Mr. J?" Ernie winked at him in the rear view mirror.

Logan frowned. He described Jess to Ernie. "Was that the woman?"

Ernie did his head bobbing with a big smile.

Logan sunk back into the seat. "What did she want to know about me?" Logan tried making the question sound natural and light.

"Oh, the usual." He grinned. "How to find you. What time you'd be off work. Said she lost your phone number. She seemed like a nice girl, Mr. J. Very pretty."

"Yeah, real nice." Sounds like she's still in journalist mode, digging up more information about me. He shook his head. So much for hoping they could work out their differences. His whole body felt cold at that realization.

Logan had Ernie drop him off at the entrance to the university. If Jess was looking for him, he couldn't go to his apartment or the culinary building through the front entrances. He would try to avoid her until this competition was all over with. Then he would plan his next step after he figured out what kind of damage her story caused.

He walked slowly around the backside of the campus, his mind torn between remembering Jess's kisses and the feeling of her betrayal. He wrenched open the glass door to the back of the culinary building, and it thudded loudly against the doorstopper. Startled by the noise, Logan realized his whole body was tense. He needed to calm down before he took his frustrations out on another door. He leaned up against the wall and concentrated on relaxing.

When he had himself under control, he headed up the back stairs to his office. He needed to get his mind off Jess. Working on the competition schedule and media setup would help keep him busy.

He let himself in his office and felt something under his shoe. He lifted his foot to see a note had been shoved under his door. He picked it up and went to sit down in his chair.

Of course, it was from Jess. It just simply said 'call me'. Logan crumpled up the paper and threw it into the wastebasket. This was going to be a tough week. She knew enough about him in the short time they knew each other to find him no matter where he went. And it wasn't as if he could just stay away from the university or his job.

He leaned forward and rested his forehead onto the cold wood of his desk. What was he going to do? Whether or not he gave her more information, she had enough of a story on his family to do some major damage to his life. Although he thought his parents deserved the problems that this story would cause, he was worried for the rest of his family and friends who were innocent bystanders. And he worried about what it would do to his new life here in Seattle. He had worked hard to start over and keep a clean reputation.

It was possible he might be safe from the fallout. Maybe she would leave his name out of the article. He pulled his forehead off the desk and leaned all the way back in his chair. As he stared at the ceiling, he thought how much he was just grasping at straws. He wanted so much to go back before he had found out what Jess had done. He closed his eyes, thinking of what could have been.

But it wasn't her fault, he reminded himself. It was his fault for saying too much too soon. But he couldn't figure out how to change what had happened, or how to minimize any future damage.

He looked around at the papers on his desk. The only thing to do right now was to concentrate on the competition. He nodded to himself as he flipped through the papers. Less than a week left. He could do this.

CHAPTER SEVENTEEN

THE COMPETITION WAS only two days away, and Jess still hadn't talked to Logan. She knew he was avoiding her — but he couldn't hide forever. She had to talk to him. It was just a matter of timing. She knew he had to go to his office and the kitchens sometime and eventually back to his apartment. She had been stalking all those places, but he had managed to be gone every time. Jess had even taken to eating lunch at Enrique's hoping she would see him there.

She put the final touches on her hair and grabbed her room key. As she rode down the elevator, she mapped out her plan for the day. Even if he couldn't forgive her, she wanted to make sure he knew that she wasn't going to drag his family into the news.

All the female staff at the hotel had a crush on Logan, so it had been easy for Jess to find out more information about him. In addition to a few other places he might be found, she'd also discovered that he had been offered head chef positions in several five star restaurants across the U.S. The girls all hoped of course that he would take the offer there in Seattle. Jess knew he wouldn't take any of those offers. It just wasn't what he wanted to do.

Jess frowned. All those women would give their left arm for a date with Logan. And here she was, having enjoyed several dates with him, and then went and ruined it all for a news story. Remorse coursed through her cold as ice.

Out front, she waved down a taxi, and once again found herself at Enrique's. Instead of going in to eat lunch as she had done every day this week, Jess walked purposefully down the block and turned the corner. She found where the alleyway started and hurried past garbage cans and recycling containers. She saw the back door to the restaurant just easing closed. Whoever had exited was already down the other end of the alley where several delivery trucks obstructed her sightline.

Jess hurried down the alleyway, turned the corner, and went back around to the front of the restaurant. The taxi she just got out of was leaving with one passenger in the back seat. She was sure it had been Logan.

Frustrated that she had just missed him, she decided to walk back to the hotel. She only got a few blocks before it started to rain, and soon she was soaked to the skin. Just perfect, she thought. She bent her head against the rain and kept walking. The rain was cold and made her whole body shiver, but at least it distracted her from her failed attempt to find Logan.

Back in her hotel room, she stripped off her soaking wet clothes and took a shower to warm up. She lingered under the hot stream of water and thought about the past week.

She was just about out of options with Logan. He had been very good at avoiding her. She would just make sure she was at the competition tomorrow. He couldn't avoid that.

As for her job, she still wasn't sure what to do. She groaned as she remembered that she only had one more night here at this luxurious hotel.

After wrapping up in one of the hotel's extra fluffy towels, Jess sat down at the desk and turned on her computer. The one decision she had made today was that she was not going back home. After meeting Logan, even though he may never talk to her again, she realized there were good people here who weren't trying to hurt her. She wanted to find more of those kinds of people. And she had fallen in love with the Seattle area, even with its daily dose of rain.

Jess slipped on her pajamas. She thought of her time at Enrique's. Everyone who worked there seemed to get along well, and it looked like they really enjoyed their jobs. Logan was lucky to have such a great place to work. Almost like having a second family. She really envied that.

And yet, it was only to her that he had confided how he wasn't sure he wanted to continue cooking in restaurants.

Jess flopped down on the bed. That was another thing they had in common. Although Jess thought she wanted the journalism job at her magazine, she wasn't quite sure now. Before, her stories only affected people she didn't know personally: celebrities, politicians, cheating spouses. Those people were far removed from her everyday life. Any harm her stories did to their lives was easily justified since she wasn't close to them and never saw any fallout up close. But after seeing the look in Logan's eyes, there was no way Jess could go back to that type of reporting. Her heart had broken as she watched the betrayal and hurt cross his face.

Her phone chirped. She rolled over and grabbed it off the bedside table, almost dropping it. Her stomach twisted when she saw the text. It wasn't Logan. It was her editor. He expected a report in the morning. Great, one more thing she needed to deal with.

Jess could feel her anxieties grabbing hold of her. There were many things that caused her to have anxiety, but the idea that she might fail and have to return home was the biggest one. She forced herself to take deep breaths and start the 5-4-3-2-1 grounding technique she had learned years ago.

Experience had shown after she got her anxiety attacks under control, the best way to avoid total melt down was to assess her situation and take action. She sat down at the little desk and took out her computer. She was determined to give her editor something. She needed to at least justify to her magazine that sending her to Seattle was worth the cost. There was a lot to learn about the Seattle area as well as the cooking competition, so Jess would start there. She would see what kind of story she could put together. There was no way she was going back to Arizona.

She sat there the rest of the day researching and only taking a short break for dinner. Jess was confident in her writing ability — she just needed to find a news story worthy of giving to her editor, but preserving her integrity at the same time. She resolved to not write any type of story that would compromise her morals again.

CHAPTER EIGHTEEN

ON THE DAY of the competition, Logan woke up before his alarm. As he stared at the ceiling and couldn't fall back asleep, he decided to go for a run. The sun wasn't up yet, but at least it wasn't raining. He pulled on a t-shirt and a pair of shorts, and laced up his running shoes.

He worked his way around the perimeter of the university, jogging past the culinary building, and then down toward the hotel. He felt a bit risky, as he had done a good job at avoiding Jess this past week and here he was going past all the places she knew to find him. He shook his head as he passed the hotel. There was no way she'd be up at this early hour anyway. He was just being ridiculous.

On his way back, he made a loop around the auditorium building just to make sure everything was locked up. He always had a feeling right before each competition that something horrible would happen before the live show started.

Satisfied all was in order, he jogged back to his apartment. It was just starting to get light out with a low layer of gray clouds hovering over the city.

Once back at his apartment, he checked his phone for messages. There were several new ones that must've come in late last night. He braced himself for another message from Jess. Her silky voice still stirred feelings in him, and he wasn't sure he could keep avoiding her for much longer. But the messages were just from several culinary students who were helping him set up for the live broadcast. Logan sighed and deleted the messages.

He threw his phone on the bed and went to take a shower. He mentally ran through all he had to do today. Not only was he a judge for the actual cooking competition, he was responsible for hosting the show since it was being filmed live. The last couple of years it had been new and exciting for him, but this year he was tired of the attention and extra socializing it created. He just wanted to be down in the kitchens cooking, or working on his new recipes.

He got dressed and headed to his office. When he finally sat down behind his paper-covered desk, he found that he was relieved that he had so far avoided Jess. No more messages on his phone or under his door. He looked around the small space. He had been lucky as a student to have an office, and that was only because he was in charge of organizing and running the cooking competition each year. This was a privilege that he was proud of because he had earned it with his own talent and hard work, not with his family's money.

Logan finished up the rest of the arrangements by noon. He stood up and stretched. He didn't need to be at the auditorium for several hours, so he had time to grab lunch. He had avoided Enrique's all week for fear of running into Jess, but today he was really craving tacos. He decided this close to the competition it was worth the risk.

He took a cab to the restaurant where Enrique was up front to greet him. Logan smiled and followed Enrique to his favorite table.

"We've missed seeing you here all week, amigo. Even when you take time off, you usually stop by for a meal." Enrique had the most infectious smile. Logan couldn't ever be in a bad mood around Enrique.

Logan nodded. "It's a good thing the competition is tonight. I'm going through salsa withdrawal." He smiled as chips and salsa were deposited in front of him.

"Your lady friend was here every day though." Enrique winked at him.

Logan lost his appetite. "Really? Every day?"

Enrique nodded. "I thought maybe she was waiting for you. I sat her here at your usual table."

Logan closed his eyes for a moment. When he opened them, his friend looked concerned. Logan waved his hand. "It was just a miscommunication. I had more work to do each day than I anticipated. At least she got to eat your fabulous food." Logan smiled up at Enrique.

"I see. Well maybe you'll get to see her today, then." Enrique shook Logan's hand and then wandered off to the next table.

That's what I'm afraid of, thought Logan as he looked nervously toward the door.

By the time his tacos were delivered to the table, Logan had relaxed. He had finished up the basket of chips and there was no sign of Jess. He ate his tacos and paid his bill. Although he was relieved to not see her, he was disappointed at the same time. What was wrong with him? Was he already forgetting the reason he was avoiding her? It wasn't just a trivial matter they had argued over. He needed to remember that.

Logan walked back to the university. Once he reached the campus, he was stopped several times by students who wanted to talk to him about tonight's big event. He smiled through clenched teeth, anxious to get ready for the competition.

Finally, he made it back to his apartment building. Waiting for the elevator was another girl from one of the cooking classes. He turned right and pushed through the stairwell doors to avoid her. Not only was he tired of talking about the competition; he just didn't want to talk to anyone right now. He took the stairs two at a time.

He showered and changed into the black and white tuxedo that was hanging in the back of his closet. Back home his family used to attend extravagant dinners and receptions quite often, so Logan would end up getting a new tux every year as he outgrew them. He was never without a tuxedo.

He straightened his black tie in front of the mirror and thought of all the ways tonight could go wrong. When you have kitchens built onto a stage, nervous contestants, people in the audience watching, as well as the media filming, there was a lot that could happen.

Then there was Jess. Logan took a deep breath. He knew that since he hadn't seen her all week, there was a good chance she was going to show up tonight. He would just have to ignore her during the competition, so he could get through the night. As long as he stayed on or behind the stage, there was no way she could get to him — until afterwards. Logan shook his head at the image in the mirror. He would worry about what to do about Jess later, as he had too much he had to concentrate on right now.

He grabbed his keys and headed out. This time he took the elevator down because he didn't want get sweaty in his tux. As he walked toward the auditorium, he mentally catalogued all the chaos surrounding the building. He watched as the caterers carried tables and food in for the after party. He chuckled to himself. He always thought it was a weird tradition to cater a party for a cooking competition.

He smiled as two gentlemen passed him in cheap brown suits. Health department. They would check to make sure everything was sanitary and up to their standards. Logan wasn't worried about them, he knew they would pass inspection.

Logan hurried past the front entrance so he could peek around the side of the building. Two media vans sat with their satellite antennas extended high. Good, looks like they're ready for tonight.

Logan went back to the front doors. The greeters let him in and he hurried up the side stairs. He knew he stood out in the crowd, as he was the only one wearing a tuxedo. He slowly made his way around to the stage. So far everything looked good.

When he finally made it to the stage, he could see that the kitchens were all set up, and the ingredients for tonight's recipes were being placed in the fridges and freezers.

The four chefs that would be competing tonight were sitting in the front row looking very nervous. Logan went over to give them his usual pep talk. He knew what it was like to be up there on stage cooking in front of so many people, so he tried to put them at ease.

As he talked with the chefs, people started to file in and find seats around the auditorium. He found himself watching faces, longing to catch a glimpse of Jess. Before the chefs noticed his distraction, he forced his attention back to his conversation. This was shaping up to be a very long night.

CHAPTER NINETEEN

JESS TOOK HER time getting dressed for the evening. Not only was this her last night at the hotel, but she hadn't seen Logan since the coffee shop incident. He really had done a fabulous job of avoiding her. She frowned in the mirror as she tried to tame her unruly curls.

She wore her best evening dress, a sapphire blue sleeveless shift that accentuated her curves. Maybe he would be so speechless seeing her in this dress that he'd forget he was mad at her. She laughed at her reflection. Not likely, Jess.

She idly thought she should pack her bag, but as she looked around the room, she realized she didn't really have much to pack. It could wait until later.

The good thing about talking to her editor this morning (after he had stopped yelling) was that he agreed to extend her stay in Seattle by a few days. At a cheaper hotel of course, but she would take it. Anything to stay in this city longer. In return, she would write an article on the cooking competition. She had convinced him that it was a very big deal in the Pacific Northwest. This gave her a few more days to figure out what her next move was.

She smiled in the mirror and wiped lipstick off her teeth. She grabbed her keys and cell phone and headed to the elevators.

Down in the lobby people were already streaming out of the elevators, dressed up for tonight's competition. They headed outside and piled into waiting cabs and limousines. Jess was glad she decided to head over to the university early. It looked like the seating was going to fill up fast. Usually she preferred being late so she could scope out the location while blending into the crowd.

She flagged down a cab and climbed in. They followed the line of cars heading to the university. The cab smelled sweaty, and she was pretty sure someone had thrown up in the back seat recently. Not a good way to start the evening. She had the driver drop her off at the edge of the university, and she walked the rest of the way to the auditorium.

She enjoyed the fresh evening air, especially after that cab ride. She shook her head. Back home it would still be hot this time of night. She loved this place.

She found the line leading into the auditorium. It wrapped around the front of the building and down the sidewalk. At the side of the building, she noticed media trucks from two different TV stations. That was interesting. She would never have thought a cooking competition would interest the media that much. Especially to warrant two stations sending crews to cover it. She thought she was pushing her creative juices just writing one article on the competition.

Jess stepped out of line and wandered over to where the media people were busy carrying equipment inside. She found one of the crew still at the back of the trucks.

She walked over to the young man, who looked like he was trying to untangle a mess of cords. "Got quite a mess there." His bright red hair stuck out of a black ball cap.

He looked up, startled. "Oh, hi. Yes, they're just for backup but I still have to get them ready."

"I'm Jess Platten with Daily Star Magazine out of Arizona. Can I ask you a few questions about tonight's competition?" She smiled sweetly.

The knot of wires forgotten, he just nodded, staring up at her from where he sat on the truck's bumper. He looked barely out of high school.

"I'm wondering why this competition is such a big deal here. Especially to get two large media outlets to cover it live." She gestured to his truck and the competitors next to it. "I mean, back home we don't have any kind of competitions like this, so I'm just curious why it's such a big deal."

The kid, probably an intern, smiled back up at Jess. "This competition has been going on since the culinary school opened years ago. It's a local favorite. It not only puts money into the university's pockets, it benefits the local businesses as well."

"So you show up on competition night and do a story on it? And that's worth all this?" Jess thought she was missing something as she gestured at the truck.

The kid shook his head. "No, we've been doing stories on this competition for weeks. Interviews, background pieces, and of course live segments where we followed the chefs around as they prepared for tonight." He gave up on the tangled wires and shoved them into a box. He closed the van door and gestured to the building. "I really need to get back inside."

Jess nodded. She watched as he went in through the side door. How did Logan's family secret not get picked up by any of these media reporters? Logan had once been a contestant in this competition, and he must've been interviewed. After all, it hadn't taken her very long to find the gory details once she started looking.

Jess shook her head and slipped through the side door. She walked right through the crowd of media people and watched from the wings of the auditorium as they did sound and light checks.

Jess found a spot where she could stand and see out into the auditorium, but was still hidden from sight. She scanned the crowd, noticing it was starting to fill up already. She needed to find a seat soon. Over at the stage there was a commotion, and when she looked up her heart skipped a beat. Logan. He was amazingly handsome in a black and white tuxedo. His already rugged good looks were made even more striking in the tux.

Memories of kissing him tormented her as she watched him cross the stage.

Two beautiful blondes in floor length glittery evening gowns walked up just then and stood on either side of him. Jess frowned. Were these some of the many women who were after Logan? Was she too late?

Jess looked back at Logan and couldn't help but to laugh.

The expression on his face was a cross between irritation and a plastic smile about to crack. His eyes darted to the side, almost as if he expected someone to rescue him. He was trying to play the part of easygoing host, but the two women clearly annoyed him. Jess was humored more than she should've been by the situation. He was clearly uncomfortable.

When the stage crew cut the spotlight, Logan blinked and then plastered a bigger smile on his face as he noticed the crowd filling in the empty seats.

The two women wandered off stage, and with her entertainment gone for the moment, Jess decided it was time to find a seat. She made her way down the aisle and sat near the middle. She had a great view of the stage, and could still see the media staff in the wings next to the stage. She was fascinated by their preparations for the live broadcast.

Logan made his way around the stage kitchens checking all the appliances and ingredients. Media people swarmed around him as they adjusted his microphone and tested the angle of the cameras set up around the stage.

Jess watched Logan try to straighten the microphone on his lapel. She wanted to jump up on stage and adjust it for him, to be close to him again. He looked up just then and made eye contact with her. Had he known she was sitting here the whole time, or did he sense her staring at him?

She gave him a tentative smile, blushing slightly at getting caught staring. She held her breath as she waited to see what kind of reaction he was going to have.

His handsome face broke into a grin, making her whole body tingle. She grinned. He stepped forward toward the front stairs, but then stopped abruptly and frowned. His expression quickly grew dark and he turned to stalk off the stage.

Jess blinked back her confusion. What was that all about? Was he happy to see her or not? She hated that dark look in his eyes. Jess grasped her handbag tighter on her lap. How was she supposed to talk to him when he was still so angry?

Her chair was bumped from behind, jostling her from her thoughts. Jess turned to see who was being so rude, and her whole body went cold as ice. Sitting down right behind her were Logan's parents. Mrs. Jacobs gave Jess a pompous sneer, and his father rolled his eyes at her.

Jess turned back around. Breathe, she told herself. She closed her eyes. Why would they be here tonight? Didn't Logan say they were good at leaving and not coming back? Yet here they were, and sitting right behind her.

She stared straight ahead, making sure they couldn't see any sort of emotion from her. Logan had seen them sitting down. That was why his expression had darkened. She breathed a little easier knowing that the deep anger she saw in his eyes probably wasn't directed toward her. She still had hope.

The lights dimmed over the audience and she watched as Logan walked slowly to the center stage to start the evening. He looked nervous, but held on to his plastic smile like a pro. Jess was acutely aware of his parents behind her, as she knew Logan was too. He didn't look at their side of the auditorium. It was going to be a long night. She just concentrated on Logan and how handsome he looked in the tux under the bright lights.

CHAPTER TWENTY

THIS WAS ONE nightmare scenario that Logan had never imagined happening on competition night. His parents never came to anything that was important to him. And now they had suddenly decided to attend his last night as competition host? And just happened to sit right behind Jess? Logan dreaded to think about what they were up to — he knew it would not be pleasant.

But right now, he had to concentrate on getting through the competition. The cameras were rolling, and there was no getting out of his responsibilities. He had to fight his instinct to hide in the back until his parents were gone.

It was bad enough trying to figure out what to do with his feelings for Jess. He had gone back and forth all week either not wanting to ever see her again, or wanting to grab her and kiss her until they forgot what they were ever fighting about.

He knew his parents were back to pressure him about the restaurant again. It always came back to what was best for the family business. They were showing him that they would not take "no" for an answer. Now Logan had even less time to figure out what he wanted to do. If he didn't come up with something soon, there was every possibility they would wear him down and he'd give in and go back with them.

He finally got to the point in the show where the chefs were cooking their dishes with no more commentary needed. The media would show clips of interviews done earlier of each chef, so Logan had an opportunity to escape to the back for a few minutes.

He made sure to stay out of sight so no one could come up and talk to him. The last thing he needed was to have to deal with anyone else. He mentally went over the new recipes he wanted to try when he got home. This always calmed him and helped him to focus. Did Jess cope in a similar way when she was writing? Did her writing help her to stay calm and focused?

The stage manager gave Logan the five-minute warning. He straightened his tux and looked out over at the chefs concentrating on plating their dishes, sweaty and nervous. At least he was only the host tonight – he had judges that would do the tasting and scoring part. He was familiar with each of these chefs, and they were all very good in the kitchen. It would be a hard choice for the judges to make.

Logan walked out on stage and finished up the evening without looking over at his parents or Jess. He knew he'd have to deal with them all sometime tonight, but he hoped he'd get a chance to talk to Jess first.

After he congratulated the winner, the spotlights went down. The crowd's clapping was thunderous. His stage manager congratulated him and started directing the cleanup crew.

As the audience filed out of their seats, Logan took a deep breath and headed toward the stairs. Above the raucous crowd, he heard a loud, harsh voice. With a groan, he looked toward the seats where Jess and his parents had been.

There his dad stood over Jess yelling at her, while waving his arms wildly.

Logan took the stairs two at a time, anger brewing. But before he could get make it through the crowd, he saw Jess turn and push her way to the side entrance. She was in tears.

"Jess!" Logan knew there was no way for her to hear him through all the racket. He hurried along the row she had taken when she disappeared. As he passed his parents, he glared at them and ignored their pleas to stop. His dad tried to grab his shoulder, but Logan ripped away and continued after Jess.

The side door was clogged with men and women carrying camera and sound equipment. By the time he got outside, Jess was nowhere to be found. He ran to the front of the building where the crowd was just starting to spill out and into the waiting cabs and limousines. Logan ran along the sidewalk. Up at the front of the line he saw Jess getting into a cab and drive off. Logan cursed and looked around. Now what?

He spotted an empty cab just pulling up, and flagged it down. When he got in, he hesitated. Where would she go? The driver asked for his destination. On a hunch, he instructed the driver to take him to the hotel where Jess was staying.

Logan sat back in the seat. His phone vibrated, and he fumbled in his pocket for it. Hope turned into anger as he saw it was his father's number lighting up the screen. He punched ignore and put it back in his pocket. What had his parents said to Jess to make her cry? They didn't even know about the article she was writing, and yet they still seemed to find something mean to throw at her.

Logan realized he had gone from being angry and upset at Jess to being worried about her and wanting to hold her and make sure she was all right. Just seeing her there with his dad hovering over her was enough to make Logan feel insanely protective of her. It made him remember the amazing days he had spent with her. He was so torn. He wanted her more than ever. But her decision to write a story on his family seemed to have destroyed their possibility of a relationship. Logan rubbed his face with his hand. Right at the moment, he didn't care about anything except making sure she was all right.

The driver let him out at the hotel. On the elevator ride up he tried to figure out what to say to Jess once he found her. He shook his head at his reflection in the mirror-covered walls. In the tuxedo he looked more confident than he felt.

Once up to her floor, he walked down and stood in front of her door. What if she was now mad at him for whatever his parents had said? He should've asked them what they had done before barging over here.

He gritted his teeth and knocked loudly. He would find out one way or another.

Silence.

He knocked again. "Jess, it's Logan."

Silence.

"I know you're in there, Jess." At least, he hoped she was.

He heard footsteps coming toward the door and breathed a sigh of relief.

"You need to go away, Logan," said Jess through the door in a small voice tainted with tears.

"I'm not going anywhere, Jess, until we talk." He paused. "Isn't that what you've been wanting to do all week?"

"So you did get my messages?"

"Yes, I'm sorry I've been avoiding you. I just wasn't sure what to say to you after — after I found out about the article."

Silence.

Logan leaned his forehead on the door. "I just want to know you're all right. I saw my father yelling at you. I have no idea what they were doing there tonight, and I'm sorry for whatever he said."

He heard Jess sniffle. "They're here to bring you back home. They pretty much told me to leave you alone because of what a dark piece of trash I am."

Logan groaned and pulled away from the door. His heart ached just thinking about her listening to those awful words from his parents. "Please, Jess. Let me in."

She half-heartedly laughed. "Guess they didn't know we hadn't even seen each other since last week. That would've made them happy."

"Jess. I'm so sorry. You don't deserve any of that."

Her sniffling stopped. Logan stood still, listening to see if she was still there on the other side of the door.

The door opened, and Jess stood aside to let him in.

Instead of going past her, Logan stepped inside and closed the door behind him. He pulled Jess to his chest in a tight hug. He leaned her against the wall, and pulled away enough to look into her eyes. They were slightly bloodshot from crying, but they still made his heart melt. She looked like she was going to cry again so he pulled her toward him and kissed her firmly. She responded by deepening the kiss, her arms going around his waist. Logan's whole body tingled. His hands caressed the bare skin on her back. Her dress fit her curves nicely and Logan's heart rate increased, as their kisses grew more heated.

Logan pulled away, putting some distance between them. He didn't want to pressure her into more than she was ready for. "You are so beautiful, Jess. I really am sorry for my parents, and for ignoring you this past week."

Jess looked up at him with a smile.

He wanted to kiss those lips again, but he restrained himself.

"You still like me this much, even after what happened between us? Even after you found out about my research?"

Logan put his hands on her hips and pulled her to him. "Yes. I've realized I don't care what happens with the story. It's only a matter of time before someone finds out the whole truth anyway. This past week showed me that I'd rather spend my time with you than covering up my family's secrets."

She frowned, and Logan's eyes went back to her lips. He wrapped his arms around her, closing any distance that remained between them. She leaned in to kiss him, and Logan's heart soared as their kisses took the heat between them to a new level. Logan tried to memorize every inch of her, how her skin felt against his, how her kisses felt against his lips, and how her perfume mixed in with the jasmine scent of her shampoo. Soon his tux and her dress were lying in heaps on the hotel room floor.

CHAPTER TWENTY-ONE

JESS HAD NEVER felt so completely caught up in someone else. For once, she wasn't afraid of getting hurt. She soon forgot about her job, the competition, and Logan's parents. It was just the two of them.

Everything else faded away.

Hours later as they lay side by side, Jess remembered she hadn't told him yet what she so desperately had tried to all week.

She rolled over to face him. His intense desire for her still took her breath away. "Logan, I've been trying to talk to you all week, not only to apologize for what I did, but to tell you something."

He caressed her bare shoulder, his touch making it hard for her to think, but she kept going. She'd waited all week for this moment.

She looked into his amazingly blue eyes. "I've decided not to do the story."

His hand stilled, and he propped himself up on his elbow. "What do you mean?"

"I mean I'm not going to write the story about your family. It was wrong of me to violate your trust that way."

His hand continued moving down Jess's shoulder. She shivered. "That's great, Jess. What will you do for a story then? You don't want to go back to writing for gossip columns."

"I don't know. I'll figure out something." She looked away, not wanting him to see how part of her regretted letting such a career-changing story go.

Logan pulled her next to him again and wrapped her in his embrace. He buried his face into her neck. "Thank you, Jess. That means a lot to me. I'm sorry you're going to miss out on your big story though."

She pulled back and looked at him, studying every beautiful line of his face. "My editor did give me a small article to write. It will at least make up for the expenses on this trip." Hopefully.

"Really?" Logan frowned.

She laughed. "I'm writing about the competition. I talked to someone with one of the news stations, and it seems your competition gets a lot of attention every year. I convinced my editor to run a story on it to encourage our local culinary schools to start something like it."

Logan moved his hands lower down her back, sending more shivers up her spine. His voice was husky when he finally answered. "That's a great idea, Jess."

Jess leaned in to kiss him, just as the hotel phone beside the bed rang. Jess gave Logan a confused look, and he just shrugged. She leaned over his bare chest to answer. "Hello?"

"There are two people down here looking for you." Jess frowned at the quiet, hurried voice.

She looked at Logan as she hung up the receiver. "I'm pretty sure your parents are waiting downstairs for you."

A cloud of anger rolled over his face.

"How did they know you were here?" Even as she asked the question, she knew the answer. Anyone with enough money could get any kind of information desired. How many people had she herself stalked, buying information for her stories?

Logan leaned back in the bed, his arms over his head, a wrinkle forming between his eyebrows as he stared at the ceiling.

"Logan? Don't you think you should get dressed and go down there?" Jess gathered the sheet around her.

He looked at her, frowning. "They intend to take me back with them. I haven't talked with them yet, so I'm not sure why they're being so pushy this time. Normally they would've just sent me a plane ticket. When they talked to you today, did you say anything about the story you were researching?"

Jess shook her head. "No. I haven't told anyone except you. They didn't give me a chance to say anything. They seemed very concerned about getting you away from me." Jess paused. "But they did specifically mention they needed you home by tomorrow." She hopped out of the bed and dug into her suitcase to find a pair of jeans and t-shirt. After she dressed, she went to her laptop, an idea forming.

"Are you packing already?" Logan sat on the edge of the bed.

Jess looked down at the suitcase. "Yes, this is my last night here."

"Then where do you intend to go?"

Jess shook her head as she typed in her password. "I don't know yet. I just know this is the last night my editor would pay for at this hotel." She was careful not to look up at him. Not only because he was very distracting sitting on the edge of her bed naked, but also because he wouldn't understand how embarrassed she was to admit she was out of money.

She heard movement behind her, but concentrated on opening up her Internet connection. She checked her emails and scrolled through the news sites.

Logan came up behind her and leaned over her shoulder, his breath hot against her neck. She dared to glance to the side and noticed he was wearing his tux again.

"Did you find anything interesting?" He ran his fingers through her hair - again very distracting.

She smiled, a shiver going up her spine. "Maybe."

"Are you going to keep me in suspense? Or should I work it out of you?" He trailed his hands around her neck and down the front of her shirt, giving her goose bumps.

"Okay, okay. If you keep doing that I won't be able to say anything."

He chuckled and stepped away long enough to drag one of the other chairs next to her. This gave her time to compose herself.

Once he was settled and her hormones were under control, Jess opened up one of the news stories she had found. "It seems your parents are coming under legal scrutiny."

"That's nothing new. They're always being sued by other companies, human rights groups, or even non-profit organizations." His tone was bitter.

Jess pointed to the screen. "But this one is different. This one is coming from the government. It seems someone, other than me, has been doing some digging into that incident years ago."

Logan went very still next to her as he read the article over her shoulder. She turned her head so she could read his expression, and saw anger mixed with fear.

"Are you all right, Logan? What does this all mean?"

"It means my parents want me home where they can keep me quiet about what happened. I must be the only loose end left, and they expect the state to come for me as a witness against them."

"I'm surprised they allowed you to finish the competition then, instead of just sweeping you away last week." Jess flipped through other articles that spelled out the charges against Logan's parents. Even if she had decided to run the article, it looked like she would've been too late. Someone had beaten her to it.

Logan got up and paced in the small room. "They tried. They even had a plane ticket ready for me. But for once I stood my ground and told them I was finishing my schooling." He stopped by the bed. "But then why did they come tonight instead of after my graduation tomorrow?"

Without turning to look up, Jess answered. "Because it says here that the state expects to have live testimony tomorrow." She turned toward Logan. "Have you received any phone calls from any government officials?"

Logan looked embarrassed. "I really haven't checked my voicemails since before the competition."

Jess smiled. "Of course. Because you were avoiding me." She closed her computer and walked over to him. As she walked into his waiting arms, for a moment she just enjoyed the beating of his heart.

Reluctantly, she pulled away far enough to look up at him. "We should listen to those voicemails before the state sends out their army or whatever security they have to come get you."

"Yes, I guess I should. I'd also like to change my clothes before I have to deal with my parents." Logan frowned. "But if my parents are downstairs, they won't leave without me. In fact I'm surprised they haven't barged in here already."

Jess smiled. She was grateful for all the lessons she had learned being a professional stalker. After staying there for several days, she knew the hotel inside and out. She grabbed his hand and headed toward the door. "They haven't come upstairs yet because the front desk clerk is buying us some time. I helped him get a date with one of the kitchen girls."

Logan closed the door behind them. "Seriously? You really know how to make friends quickly." He smiled down at her.

They got in the elevator, and Jess pushed the button for the third floor.

"Third floor? How is that going to help us?" Logan looked nervous.

"On the third floor there is a back stairwell to the kitchens. We can get outside without ever having to go through the front." She winked at him.

Logan visibly relaxed and Jess was tempted to kiss him all over again. The elevator doors opened on the third floor just then, keeping her from acting on impulse. They headed toward the stairwell, hand in hand.

CHAPTER TWENTY-TWO

AFTER WALKING THE three flights down, they ducked into the kitchen. Jess thanked and hugged a short blond girl for her help. Logan felt awkward because even though he had lived in Seattle for years, he only knew the people who worked at the hotel by sight. But they all seemed to know who he was, and they all knew and loved Jess. Another reason Logan felt so drawn to Jess – she genuinely cared about people and made friends easily. He understood completely why she had issues writing gossip pieces, because she got too attached to her sources.

Once safely back inside his apartment, Logan started to relax.

"Are you hungry?" He looked over and found that she looked quite at home on his couch. He grinned, temporarily forgetting about food.

"The voicemail first." She smiled and pointed to the counter where his phone was charging.

Logan knew he was delaying. He picked up the phone and dialed his voicemail. There were a few messages from Jess. He smiled as he heard her voice. Then a few messages from his parents, which he deleted. Finally he came to a message from the South African state investigator. Logan listened carefully as the man asked him to call, and wrote the number down on a sticky note.

"Well?" Jess came to stand next to him. He smiled as his body responded to her closeness. He wanted nothing more than to pick her up and take her to his bedroom and forget about the mess they were dealing with.

He ran a hand through his hair. "They called." He held up the note. "Left a number for me to call. You're right, they need my testimony tonight."

"And?"

"And, I'm not sure what to do. He said they have all the evidence they need to bring charges against my parents, but the state wants my testimony to seal the case. Not surprisingly, evidence and witnesses seem to be disappearing. "

"And if you don't testify against them?" Jess frowned.

"Then they will include me in the charges." Logan closed his eyes and leaned back against the counter. "But even if I were to testify, I don't see how I can before my parents find me."

"Would your parents really try to remove you by force?"

He nodded, dark images swarming in his head. "You've seen the news reports. It was worse in person. It doesn't matter that I'm their son. They'll do anything to save themselves."

Logan felt Jess's arms come around him and she leaned her body against his. He opened his eyes to her smiling face.

"I have an idea." She leaned up and kissed him. He put his arms around her and continued the kiss.

Jess broke off the kiss with a gentle laugh. "That was nice, but that wasn't my idea." She drew away. "It sounds like you need to testify whether you want to or not." She waited until Logan nodded. "Do your parents know where you live?"

"They've only been to my office. But if they don't already know, it won't take them long to find out where I am." He frowned. This is exactly why he'd always been cautious of letting people get to close to him. "You need to leave before they get here."

"Nope. We're both going to get out of here. Grab your phone. We'll go someplace safe where you can call the investigator back. Once your parents are in jail, they can't do anything to you. Right?"

Logan'd had all sorts of bad thoughts toward his parents while he was growing up. He had wished they were in plane accidents, or that he would find out he was really adopted. But was he ready to be the one to put them behind bars? To Jess he said, "I think once I testify, they won't be able to hurt me again."

Jess nodded. "I'm sorry, Logan. I'm sorry for what they did to your friends, and for all you're going through now." She stepped back.

Logan grabbed his phone and keys and walked ahead of Jess to the door so she wouldn't see the tears welling up in his eyes. He made sure there wasn't anyone in the hallway and hurried toward the stairwell. He looked back at her, more composed now. "Ready for more stairs?"

She smiled at him. "Going down is easy."

They didn't say much as they descended to the garage level. Logan didn't want to take the chance of meeting up with his parents in the main foyer.

He took Jess's hand as they walked across the quiet garage. There were a few cars parked in stalls, but no one came or left while they were there. "Now what, Jess?"

"Now you call your friend Ernie and have him pick us up a few blocks away from here."

Logan wasn't even surprised she remembered the cab driver's name. "Then what? They might have people at the hotel looking for us still."

She squeezed his hand. "I have an idea. You just get us a ride and then I'll take care of the rest."

After Logan told Ernie where to pick them up, they hurried off campus to meet him. They stayed off the sidewalks since Logan was still in his tux and would be easily spotted. He should've changed when they were at his apartment.

Once they were in Ernie's cab, Jess gave him an address she had pulled up from her phone. Logan was too tired to ask Jess where they were going. He just leaned his head back and closed his eyes. Jess scooted close to him and interlaced their fingers. He smiled but otherwise didn't move.

When the cab came to its final stop, Logan opened his eyes and started to get out. When he saw the sign on the building, he froze in place. "Why are we here, Jess?"

She pushed him the rest of the way out of the cab so they were both standing on the sidewalk in front of a news studio. "How else are you supposed to give your deposition when the government investigator is over ten thousand miles away?"

Logan turned toward Jess. "I guess I figured I would just talk to them over the phone."

She shook her head, curls bouncing around her face. He had a sudden urge to weave his fingers through her hair, but she grabbed his hand and pulled him toward the door. "Come on. They can video tape you while you answer the government official's questions."

"I don't know about this, Jess. I've been trying to avoid the media. Now you want me to basically tell them everything?"

Jess put her other hand on her hip and looked hard at him. "It's already in the news, Logan. This way you'll have public protection. Your parents don't know where we are, and soon you will have witnesses and video evidence that they can't get rid of. And everyone will know your side of the story. Did you know that some of those news stories tied you into the mess? You don't want to take the fall for your parents."

Logan could see the journalist in Jess coming out. He smiled. "You're good at this, you know that?" He let go of her hand so he could put his arm around her.

"You mean talking men into spilling their family secrets onto the evening news?" Jess was joking, but Logan could tell there was an undercurrent of hurt.

He stopped and pulled her to him. "No, that's not what I meant. I'm talking about how you know how to use whatever resources you find around you to make a bad situation better." He kissed the top of her head.

"Oh. I guess all those years of being a gossip reporter weren't wasted then." She smiled up at him.

He waved a hand at the sign lit up above them. "You know, this will be a very big story for you."

"What do you mean?"

"I mean if I do this, I want you there with me. This will be your exclusive story, the one on one with the golden boy who worked with the government to take down his corrupt parents." Logan tried to make it sound light, but his words caught in his throat. As much as his parents deserved whatever punishment awaited them, they were still his parents. This was a situation no child should be put in.

Jess's eyes seemed to take in every emotion Logan tried to hide. She leaned up and kissed him with so much passion that Logan nearly did cry right then. He hugged her tight to his chest. He could do this, with her help. He had run long enough. It was time to do what he should've done years ago.

CHAPTER TWENTY-THREE

JESS'S HEART HURT for the Logan and the dilemma he faced. What he was about to do would be hard for him. She smiled up at him, noticing his eyes were full of unshed tears.

"Thank you, Jess for being here with me."

"Thank you for trusting me, Logan." She was going to cry too if they didn't get this over with. She blinked the moisture away. "I'm just glad it wasn't me that broke this news story."

Logan nodded and smiled. He opened the door and they stepped into the studio.

At the front desk, Jess asked for the young cameraman whom she had talked to earlier at the competition. She hoped that she wouldn't have to do too much persuading to enlist his help. The front desk girl looked at Jess in confusion as she called back into the studio.

Jess wandered over to the wall where awards the station had won were displayed behind glass frames. The station had earned most of the major awards, including the Edward R. Murrow award. Jess was impressed that such a small studio was putting out such quality programming.

"Hello?"

Jess turned around to see the young redhead walking into the lobby. When he saw her, a flash of recognition passed over his features, and he grinned. "I remember you from outside the event tonight near our truck. I'm sorry, I didn't catch your name." He extended a hand.

Jess shook his hand. "I'm Jess Platten. And I'm sure you know Mr. Jacobs." Jess gestured to Logan.

"Yes, sure." He looked back and forth between Jess and Logan. "I'm Jerry Thompson. So I hear you want to talk to me? Did I do something wrong tonight?"

"No, you didn't do anything wrong, Jerry. Can we talk somewhere privately?" Jess added in a low voice. "It's very important and I promise we won't be wasting your time."

Jerry looked like he wanted to ask more questions, but he just shrugged and showed them through the studio. He led them into a conference room with two walls that were floor to ceiling glass and a massive black oval table in the center surrounded by plush chairs.

Jerry shut the door and they all sat down. He looked at Jess expectantly.

Jess looked over at Logan before she started. "We're here because we need you to tape a deposition for us. The information you'll hear tonight will need to be kept secret for a few days, until the court has time to enter it into their records and file the charges."

Jerry just stared at her, looking even more confused.

Jess continued, "But after that time, we'll be able to use the information as a news story. A very big news piece that gives Logan's side of a story that is already making international headlines. I will be the lead journalist on the breaking story, but if you help us with this, your name will be connected as the main photo journalist." She watched Jerry digest the information.

He looked at Logan. "You're the one who needs the deposition? And when did you want to do this?"

"Yes, my parents are part of the Cape May scandal. And we need to do this tonight. As soon as possible." He held up his cell phone. "The prosecutors for the government in South Africa are waiting for me to call them back."

Jerry's eyes grew wide. "South Africa? Tonight? I just got back from taping the competition. I haven't even unpacked the van yet." He looked at Jess. "And I don't have the authority to do this. I would need to find my boss and explain it to her."

Jess nodded. "I understand it's very short notice, but this is an emergency. I'm sure your boss would understand. Why don't you find her for us, and we'll call the prosecutor and see how they want to set this up." She looked around the scarce room wondering if they would have to film here.

"You're really serious." He frowned. "Okay, let me go get her." He held his hands up as he got up from his chair. "Just stay here and I'll be right back."

Jess nodded at him, amused. Once Jerry left, she turned back to Logan. "When you call them back, let them know that we have a way to video tape it with witnesses in the room. See how many questions they have for you so we can let Jerry and his boss know about how long it will take."

Logan looked nervous, but he dialed his contact at the prosecutor's office. He cleared his throat. "Hello? Mr. Han? It's Logan." Logan pressed his lips together as he listened.

Jess couldn't hear what was being said on the other end of the call. Logan explained where they were and what they were doing. The other person must've approved of their idea because Logan was soon smiling.

After he hung up the phone, he programmed another phone number into his phone. "He gave me another phone number to call in fifteen minutes. They're getting set up to record on their end as well."

Jerry stepped into the room with a very tall and thin gray-haired woman. "I'm Alice Emerson," she said as she walked forward to shake Logan and Jess's hands. "Jerry here tells me you have a big story for us?"

Jess pulled up one of the news articles about Logan's parents on her phone. She put it in front of Alice. "This news story has already hit the foreign news media outlets, but it will hit ours by morning. Logan needs to give his side of the story for the prosecutors so they can file charges against his parents."

Alice's eyes grew wide, and she looked hard at Logan. "Your parents?" He nodded. "And you're testifying against them?"

He nodded. "They did horrible, unspeakable things to innocent people. It's time they paid for what they've done." Logan looked away, a solemn look on his handsome face.

Jess wanted to throw her arms around him to give what comfort she could, but she knew that would have to wait. Instead, she asked Alice, "Will you help us? We need to call the prosecutor back in fifteen minutes. He will ask Logan all the questions. It's early tomorrow morning down there, so he needs this video before noon their time so he can submit it to the court before the end of their business day."

Alice looked between Jerry, who was standing on the other side of Logan, and Jess. Jerry smiled and nodded. She sighed and said, "Yes, we can do this. I want the station to have exclusive rights to his story." She pointed her manicured finger at Jess. "But I will concede that you can get credit for the story as well, and written rights." She looked at Logan. "I'll print off some legal stuff for you to sign while Jerry sets up the small studio for recording." She looked at Jerry who grinned and hurried out of the door.

"Thank you, Alice, for doing this for us." Jess took Logan's hand and they followed Alice through the newsroom to an office in the back. Logan and Jess signed papers and filled Alice in on the whole story. When it was about time to call the prosecutor back, the three of them headed to the recording studios at the back of the building. As they traipsed by newsroom desks, equipment rooms, and high tech equipment, Jess thought that it seemed like a nice place to work. Maybe she could find a job at a news station like this. She smiled to herself in determination as they were ushered into a room set up with a desk and several cameras.

They got Logan settled in front of the cameras, and the prosecutor on speakerphone. The prosecutor went through all of his questions and Jess's heart broke all over again as she heard the first hand details from Logan. As he haltingly answered each question, Jess could see the devastation of the village in her mind.

Several hours later they wrapped up, the prosecutor reminding Logan that at some time in the future he might need to come back to South Africa to speak to the judge in person if there were more questions. Jess hoped that wouldn't happen, but she knew that Logan had already gone through the hard part.

When the cameras and microphones were turned off, Logan stood up and walked out without saying anything. Jess started to follow, but Alice put her hand out to stop her.

"Let him decompress for a few minutes, Jess. And besides, I would like to talk to you." She spoke to Jerry for a few minutes, and then led Jess back to her office.

CHAPTER TWENTY-FOUR

LOGAN SHOOK THE dean's hand and walked down the stairs on the other side of the stage. He grinned as he sat back down next to the most beautiful woman he had ever known. Jess gave him a kiss on the cheek and squeezed his hand as they watched the rest of his class accept their certificates.

Although he was physically and mentally exhausted from staying up late the night before taping the deposition against his parents, Logan felt light and complete today. The past could no longer haunt him. He was now free to do anything, go anywhere he wanted to, without worrying about whether or not people would find out about the tragedy in South Africa. The world now knew what had happened to those beautiful people near Cape May.

He looked sideways at Jess. Best of all, there were no more trust issues between him and Jess. He had asked her to move in with him until they could figure out where they wanted to settle down. For now, the university had asked him to stay and teach advanced cooking classes for another year. That would give him more time to figure out where he wanted his career to go. After the taping last night, Alice had asked Jess if she wanted to work for her as a staff writer. Jess eagerly accepted, not even bothering to ask about pay. Logan smiled, remembering Jess's face glowing with joy.

After the graduation ceremony, Logan hustled Jess to the waiting taxi. Ernie laughed at them as they tumbled into the back seat grinning like teenagers.

"You know what every great celebration needs?" Logan kissed the tip of Jess's nose.

She pretended to look thoughtful. "Shopping?"

Logan laughed and sat back in the seat. "Tacos of course. And flan. Don't you think that would be the perfect ending for this day?"

She nodded. "Absolutely. Tacos make everything better."

Jess looked radiant in the emerald summer dress she wore. Logan almost asked Ernie to take them home, but he knew there would be plenty of time for that. He grinned and kissed her again.

***

JESS FELT LIKE she was in some sort of alternate reality where she was happy, safe, and in the arms of the most handsome, caring man she had ever imagined. Every time he touched or kissed her, she was reminded that this was real, not just a dream. This was really happening.

They got out of the taxi and headed into Enrique's. They sat at Logan's usual table and started in on chips and salsa.

Jess had already called her editor that morning and told him she wasn't coming back to Arizona. He had several choice words for her and told her he was confident she would come crawling back eventually. She had hung up and emailed her story about the competition to him with an official notice of resignation. It had felt good to do that.

For once, Jess didn't feel anxious about her actions. Alice's job offer had been a surprise, and it thrilled Jess all the way down to her toes. No more gossip columns. She would be writing regular news stories from now on.

Jess smiled as she watched Logan sitting across from her. He was talking animatedly to Enrique as he tried to get the flan recipe from his friend. Good-hearted banter went back and forth between them as waiters and hostesses hurried to serve the crowd of hungry customers around them.

Jess took a deep breath and let it out. This would be part of her life now, going places with Logan and not having to worry about staking out the entrances and staff first. Soft laughter bubbled up. She had learned that she didn't have to choose either Logan or her career – she could have both. Jess had finally found the place where she belonged, here in the emerald city of Seattle.

The end

ACKNOWLEDGEMENTS AND A RECIPE!

Although *The Perfect Story* is fictional, there really is an Enrique's Mexican Restaurant that serves the best authentic Mexican food you will ever taste, in Kuna, Idaho.

I am truly blessed to count the owners, Enrique and Ana as close friends and family. They are the most generous, caring, and charismatic people I have ever known. I am thankful to them for allowing me to use their restaurant as an inspiration for this novella.

AND they gave me their amazing Flan recipe to share with all my readers! Please check out the recipe on the next page and enjoy!

Heather J. James is the pen name for the romance novellas that Heather Lee Dyer writes. Sign up on the website below to get information when new YA novels or A Dash of Romance novellas will be published.

www.heatherleedyer.com

Twitter: @HeatherLeeDyer_

Facebook: www.facebook.com/heatherleedyer

Enrique's Flan Recipe

12 Eggs
2 cans Condensed Milk
4 cans Milk (use the same can from the condensed milk to measure)
1 cup Sugar
1 splash Vanilla (use the lid of the vanilla)
1 dash Cinnamon
2 drops Egg Shade food coloring
2 oz. Coffee Liquor

Mix all the ingredients together with a whisk, except for the sugar.

Place the sugar in a saucepan on low heat, stirring until it turns into caramel. Once you have the consistency you need, immediately poor into container where flan will be formed. Make sure to spread the caramel evenly on the entire surface.

Pour the ingredients mixed earlier over the caramel.

Cook using the water bath method for 1½ hours at 350 degrees. Let it cool for 6 hours. Separate the flan from the bowl with a knife going around all the edges. Place the tray over the flan pan, grab it firmly then flip over quickly so flan lies on tray. Top with whipped cream and a cherry.

Enjoy!

www.enriqueskuna.com